July 30, 2019
To Lisa and
The beautiful
Woodward
sisters!
(p. 102)
Bvon
Appetito!
xo.
Valerie
Caccia

# HOW TO *eat*
# A MILLENNIAL
*.. one byte at a time*

**Valerie Caccia**

authorHOUSE®

AuthorHouse™
1663 Liberty Drive
Bloomington, IN 47403
www.authorhouse.com
Phone: 1 (800) 839-8640

Artist: Kelly Jackson
www.kellyportfolio.com
Photographer: Steve Tacang
Correction Consultant: Gem Carvey

This is a work of fiction. All of the characters, names, incidents,
organizations, and dialogue in this novel are either the products
of the author's imagination or are used fictitiously.

© 2019 Valerie Caccia. All rights reserved.

No part of this book may be reproduced, stored in a retrieval system, or
transmitted by any means without the written permission of the author.

Published by AuthorHouse  03/08/2019

ISBN: 978-1-5462-7786-6 (sc)
ISBN: 978-1-5462-7785-9 (hc)
ISBN: 978-1-5462-7883-2 (e)

Library of Congress Control Number: 2019901217

Print information available on the last page.

This book is printed on acid-free paper.

Because of the dynamic nature of the Internet, any web addresses or links contained in
this book may have changed since publication and may no longer be valid. The views
expressed in this work are solely those of the author and do not necessarily reflect the
views of the publisher, and the publisher hereby disclaims any responsibility for them.

For my mother, Marilynn, my editor and best friend.

For my late father and soulmate, R. Frank, whose words inspire me to this very day.

For our First Responders, victims, and everyone touched by the wildfires in the beautiful state of California.

For Connors, who told me, "Keep the dog."

With Special Thanks to a millennial named Prince who sold me a magic printer.

# CONTENTS

# CONTENTS

# INTRODUCTION
## *A Truly Authentic Story*

I am 53 years old and that makes me Generation X.

I could listen to Tony Bennett's "I Left My Heart in San Francisco", every single night of my life. If you are a millennial, please keep reading. It is, what it is.

If you haven't heard about me or read anything I've written, it's probably because I haven't written anything in about 30 years. One millennial lifetime.

I am NMNK. Never Married, No Kids. People are always saying to me, "Oh, Val, you have no kids." I say, "Oh, no, don't feel sorry for me. I have your kids. An entire generation of kids that I would love to sit down and talk with."

I mean that, sincerely.

I was young once. I was a high achiever. I understand the fun in living large and living for today.

I like being older. It's a mindset. The journey is truly part of the gift.

Every generation's point of view matters. Intergenerational connectivity and how we relate to each other is important. In this time of great sharing, I thought I would participate and share my point of view.

I sell real estate for a living, which was supposed to be a means to an end. My end game, my dream, was to write.

If I told a millennial that I had a dream at 53, they would probably say, "Next!" Well, at least that's what I thought they'd say. I didn't know.

Over the course of nine weeks, the time it took me to write this book, I met, talked to, and spent time with a lot of millennials. When I told them I had a dream, they asked me what it was.

They were not rude. They did not dismiss me. In fact, they were quite the opposite.

When the digital natives found out I was a San Francisco native, they wanted a selfie with me. I was like an endangered species. They hopped and jumped, "Look! We found one!" I became the challenge on their team treasure hunt. I was helping them bond.

My transaction coordinator is a millennial named Logan. We didn't always understand one another like we do today. I remember when we did our first deal together. I tried to explain what life was like when I was growing up and he asked me to hang on while he sent documents via Dropbox to our seller from his iPhone.

This was not my life as I envisioned it.

When did my generation become so irrelevant? When did the kid's table take over the dining room?

Now there's an even younger Generation Z. Who will these people be? How will they relate to us? I was unloading groceries from my car the other day and a middle-schooler rode by me on his bicycle and screamed, "What up, MILF?"

My mother, the Silent Generation, stood there silently. What must she think of all of this? God bless her. My mother is 80 years old and extremely astute, but she has a lot of questions.

Last week, I tried to explain to her, that the young person behind the counter at our local pharmacy identifies as a man, so although she looks like a woman, my mother should be respectful and just call her Jake.

At that point, my mother stopped identifying with me.

The purpose of this book is to share my perspective through brand storytelling and creative content. You may not agree with my point of view, but I hope you will open your minds to it.

IMHO, the world needs to laugh.

As far as laugh making credentials go, when I was millennial age, I did stand-up comedy. I performed at the Holy City Zoo and Bimbo's 365 Club in San Francisco; The Comedy Store and The Pasadena Playhouse in Southern California.

I studied screenwriting under Bob Merrill at Loyola Marymount University in Los Angeles and am the author of "Comedienne-apause", a concept sought-after by Joan Rivers.

My employment with Neil Simon was an amazing experience.

I remember years ago, interviewing with Hollywood agent, Sue Mengers, to see if she would hire me for a staff position in her office because I needed a job. Sue asked me what I wanted to do, and I told her I wanted to write. Sue asked, "So, what are you doing here?" With that, she marched me out of her office, looked me straight in the eyes and said, "Valerie, go home and write." And she closed the door.

It took me a while, but I finally did it.

A wise woman, from a generation older than mine, told me you have two choices in life. You can cry or you can laugh. I choose to laugh.

I hope you enjoy my startup book. I hope it makes you laugh.

---
▼
---

# MILLENNIAL LANGUAGE LEARNING, CAN I EVEN DO IT?

The first time I called my hair salon and heard the word "reservationist" on their recording, something inside me died.

"Please hold and a reservationist will be with you shortly."

There was an incoming call on my mobile phone. It was Logan. I answered, "Hi, Logan. I'm having a moment. What's up?"

"Nothing. I'm just checking on you. What's the problem?"

"I was just trying to make a hair appointment."

"How did that go?"

"I hung up."

Logan laughed and asked, "Why did you hang up?"

"Have you ever heard of making a hair reservation?"

"A reservation for a haircut, yes. Why are you being so passive-aggressive over that word?"

"How is making a hair appointment passive aggressive?

"You're resisting."

"I look like Don King, that's what I'm resisting. Do you know who that is?"

"No."

"What's going on at my hair salon? What happened to Meghan, the receptionist? I liked her so much. Maybe she went back to school."

"Okay. Did you just call her a receptionist? You need to stop."

"What am I supposed to call her?"

"What did you used to call her?"

"I called her Meghan."

"Oh, I think I know her. She works at Jane.com now. Oy! Who cares? I need to go spin."

I showed up early that day. The day of my haircut reservation. I didn't trust it.

The elevator opened and there they were. The millennials. The early bird millennials. The coffee carriers, the stylists; striking down stereotypes of laziness, speaking loudly and confidently as if they were just kids and knew there was company.

They lost focus and became quiet for a moment when they spotted me. Then they started up again. I assumed they dismissed me as basic because I was wearing leggings.

I sat on the window ledge near the hanging hair cutting capes and I thought to myself, "I didn't even know hair salons had meetings. I must be old. What could they possibly be talking about?"

Their salon chairs were in a synonymous swivel. A leather bench had been moved in to create a circle. They sat poised in their talking circle and talked about mousse.

I heard the brand they were talking about and I recognized it. I could feel a bend in my knee. I wanted to jump in the circle.

They seemed like a product heavy crowd. Maybe I should just get my hair cut and move on.

The City had changed. It was all about demand-responsive parking meters, e-bikes and no plastic straws.

Come to think of it, I had changed, too. I used to run around The City in four-inch heels carrying high-end handbags. That day, I was in Nike Flyknits and wearing an RFID-travel neck wallet.

My sophisticated millennial friend, Charlie, stopped by the salon for a quick visit. The neck wallet was his E-stop.

"That is over the top!" Charlie said, "What has happened to you?! I miss your handbags!"

I directed him to Fashionphile.

Handbags have a much better resale value than shoes, for obvious reasons. I try to put myself in other people's shoes quite a bit, just not in the literal sense.

Millennials are a far more literal generation than Generation X and older generations. We tend to speak in idioms. We grew up that way. It's our generational style.

Millennials like words used in their most exact sense. Give it to them straight. Define your idiom. Say what you mean to say.

Almost every single millennial I told that I was writing a book about their generation, asked me the same honest question: "How long is it?"

The generation was endearing itself to me.

As I sat in the hair salon, my mobile phone alerted me to a new message. I went to answer the message and accidentally turned on the flashlight.

The millennial sitting next to me gave me the side-eye. He blinked it, to let me know I had flashed the light in his eye. I thought to myself, that must be the reservationist.

Where was Inclusivity when I needed her?

# INCLUSIVITY

Inclusivity lives in the Marina. Her real name is Carmel Fontina. She changed it as part of a social experiment.

Inclusivity gets along with everyone. She doesn't walk on egg-shells. She's open-minded, open-hearted and unprejudiced.

Inclusivity welcomes a challenge. In fact, instead of choosing a location for her social experiment based on its multi-culturalism and diversity, Inclusivity chose a location in Orange County, two blocks from the Fashion Island Mall.

I remember back when she was still Carmel. She called me one night in tears. She thought she was Italian, but when she did her DNA and the results came back, they didn't match her siblings. Their ancestry all came back pure northern Italian, mapped beautifully up at the top. Carmel's came back from Ecuador. It was after she read the gene mapping that she had her breakdown.

Inclusivity was born out of the need for tolerance. She didn't appreciate her older sister, Louisa, making jokes like, "This might explain why you don't like prosciutto."

Carmel was shocked by the results and hurt by her sister's insensitivity. She wondered if they were even sisters. Did she even have a family?!

She tried to reduce her stress by doing Tai Chi in Washington Square Park.

She tried to distract herself with the frescos in Coit Tower.

Eventually, Carmel retreated to her grandmother cave. Otherwise known as her full floor top flat, in a three-unit building she owned near the corner of Beach and Fillmore Streets.

Carmel's grandmother cave consisted of three things; her grandchildren, her almond raspberry filled torte, and the Hallmark Channel.

Carmel baked so much almond and raspberry torte that the local market ran out of raspberry preserves.

The millennials in their apartments didn't even notice. They made healthier choices and ate things like roasted brussel sprouts and carrot hummus from Greens.

Three weeks had passed since Carmel talked to Louisa. Despite the layers and layers of raspberry preserves Carmel had slathered on top of her hurt feelings, she was still not over it. But, her tortes were simply scrumptious.

Carmel hadn't thought of those two words together since Stonestown Galleria was an outdoor mall and had a popular coffee shop called Simply Scrumptious. She and Louisa used to meet there for coffee. They served coffee in clear glass goblets.

Carmel wanted to tell her friends about her situation, but she was worried what they would say. Then she remembered the empty sugar packet she had saved from all those years ago at coffee with Louisa. It had a quote on it from Elbert Hubbard that read: "Never explain, your friends don't need it and your enemies will never believe it anyway."

Carmel was clear about one thing. She wasn't going to become a bitter person. In fact, her generosity of spirit prevailed during this troubled time and she decided to take two of her tortes down to the schoolyard as a donation to the neighborhood bake sale.

Someone explained the millennials to her at the bake sale.

Carmel was fun-loving, mellow and ageless. She thought the millennials might be just the family she was looking for. She wondered if the millennials would accept her.

The idea for the social experiment was rooted in the roots of her questionable roots.

While watching a Peanuts cartoon with her grandchildren about a warm blanket, Carmel was reminded of her dear friend, Olga, who had recently moved to Orange County. Olga and Carmel used to sit and knit multicolored ripple afghans together, while the Blue Angels buzzed the flats. *The Wild Parrots of Telegraph Hill,* now an aviation unit in the hundreds, flew out of the trees. Those were the good old days, Carmel thought to herself.

Days later, while sweeping the sidewalk outside her flats, Carmel's baby boomer friend, Pam, pulled up in her Subaru. Pam lowered the passenger window, asked Carmel where she had been hiding and insisted she join her. They went to Ton Kiang for dim sum and saw "A Star is Born" at The Kabuki.

Pam was right. It was time to make some GOOD NEW DAYS!!

Carmel moved forward with the social experiment. She called Olga and accepted Olga's invitation to visit and stay with her.

On the morning Carmel's grandchildren left to visit their paternal grandparents in Perth for the holidays, Carmel boarded a commuter flight from SFO to the John Wayne Airport in Orange County. Although she was afraid to fly, Carmel just felt like flying and she overcame her fear. It was a smooth flight.

The experiment was to be taken seriously and conducted over a period of three weeks. It began the moment Carmel stepped off the plane, onto the moveable airstairs and set foot on Southern California soil.

Carmel met Ainsley, a millennial car rental agent, coincidentally at the Starbuck's inside the airport.

Carmel Fontina was now Inclusivity.

I called Carmel as she and Ainsley were walking to the car rental office down a long passenger walkway. It was a somewhat private conversation because Ainsley was a fast-moving millennial. Faster than Carmel, anyway.

In the experiment and in the moment, Carmel stopped

to catch her breath and answered my call, "Hello, this is Inclusivity."

"Hi, Carmel, I mean Inclusivity," I said, in full cooperation, "How are you?"

"I'm walking with my new millennial friend, Ainsley. She's going to help me rent a car," Inclusivity said, as she resumed walking.

"You have a millennial friend already?"

"Yes! I met her at Starbuck's. We were waiting in line and I figured there was no better time and place to start. So, I decided to go for it and talk to a millennial."

"You're a brave woman, Inclusivity."

"Ainsley was ordering a pink drink and I asked her, 'Is that a Millennial Pink Latte? I thought they were only selling those in Japan.' I read that in Food and Wine Magazine on the airplane."

"Is that true? Is there a Millennial Pink Latte?" I asked.

"Yes, it's true! There is a Millennial Pink Latte. Of course, Gen Z yellow is the new millennial pink," Inclusivity said.

"You've been doing your research, Inclusivity."

"I did more reading on the plane than I've done all year. Did you hear about Pixar's first female millennial director of an animated short? She wrote it, too. It's a computer-animated short film about a Chinese dumpling named 'Bao'. She won an Academy Award!"

"I haven't heard about any of this."

"It's true. I can identify with her mother not wanting to let her daughter go. I almost couldn't say goodbye to my grandchildren this morning."

"But, look! You've already made so much progress."

"I know. When I asked Ainsley about her pink drink,

11

she said she ordered it off the secret menu. It was the Pink Starburst Frappuccino. She hadn't heard about the Millennial Pink Latte either. Just like you! We're more alike than we know!"

"Oh my gosh, Inclusivity! Your experiment is working! You're breaking down social barriers, one woman at a time!"

"I know! Except, then I had a set-back. She asked me my name. When I told her Inclusivity, she asked me if I was a stripper."

There was an incoming call on my mobile phone. It was Logan.

"Inclusivity, hang on one minute," I said, switching to Logan's call, "Hi, I'm on the phone with Inclusivity."

"Oh! How's she doing?!"

"Amazing! She's already becoming a friend to the millennials."

"Stop it," Logan said, laughing.

"It's true. Who knows how many lives she will touch."

"I'm inspired!" Logan exclaimed, "I can't believe it! I didn't even think it was real when I first heard about all of this. It's all happened so fast."

"Did Bridgette call?" I asked.

"Yes. She just confirmed. That's what I called to tell you," Logan said.

"Great. Thank you," I said.

"Tell Inclusivity, I said 'Hi', and to keep up the good work!"

"I will. Ciao."

"Bye," Logan said and was gone. He always ended the call before me. How did he do that so fast?

While Inclusivity waited for her car rental, she learned

that Ainsley was ironically and completely by chance, friends with Marissa Marie, a neighbor in Olga's apartment complex.

Ainsley and Inclusivity would meet again.

Ainsley upgraded Inclusivity's car rental and welcomed her to the O.C.

As Inclusivity drove down the Pacific Coast Highway in her Mercedes-Benz GL450 Sport Utility Vehicle, she felt a sense of belonging alongside all the fancy cars with their personalized plates. The weight of the SUV going down a hill, however, was something she'd have to get used to. Inclusivity was seen backing out of two intersections on a red light.

Feeling somewhat overly confident, Inclusivity turned on the radio and raised the volume. She quickly discovered her car rental radio only received one channel. It was a rap music channel; 24/7.

Carmel would have been turned off by the profanity of the rap music and changed the vibration to no music at all, but Inclusivity shifted her thinking. Upon hearing the rawness of emotion, Inclusivity began to experience a rare form of Draking brought on by failed DNA expectations.

Inclusivity spent a lot of time in her car because that's what you do in Southern California.

Fastened with her technical truth, she listened to rap music 24/7. She tried to incorporate the new way. It was only a matter of days before Inclusivity could vocally deliver every word to the consensual version of "Baby, it's Cold Outside".

I reached out to Inclusivity the following week to see how she was doing. She told me of the many new millennial friends she had made. More specifically, Olga's two neighbors. Inclusivity found them fascinating.

The neighbor in the apartment directly next door to Olga's

was a popular bachelor millennial with a perfect fluff of hair. His name was Angaura; "Aura" with an "A-N-G". That was his signature and very successful pick-up line.

Angaura was a pillow designer. He designed pillows for the rich and famous, made from faux angora. There was nothing faux about Angaura. He was fit and living his best life. He was honest about the stage of life he was navigating and had no objection to it. Neither did the throngs and thongs of people Angaura brought back to his apartment. An apartment that was kept like a posh Manhattan penthouse, with a housecleaner and luxury home textiles. There was even breakfast cereal because they didn't have to do the dishes.

Inclusivity heard a lot of giggling and laughter through those walls. Among other things ...

One night, Angaura hosted a nonsexual cuddle party. He had pillows, but no blankets. Angaura knocked on Olga's door and asked if he could borrow some of her afghans. He invited Olga and Inclusivity to cuddle. They loaned Angaura the afghans, but respectfully declined his invitation, opting out for another fun social experience. A game of bingo. At a hipster bar.

Olga's neighbor on the opposite side was Marissa Marie, future architect to the future King of England.

Marissa Marie had her own Christmas tree in her own room to decorate as a child and would bond with the future king over that shared memory.

One day the Private Secretary to the Sovereign would call for Marissa Marie, right there on her mobile phone in Orange County. Marissa Marie would be having a lazy day playing her cello and enjoying a Froyo from Top That Yogurt. She would initially think someone was playing a prank. Then she would recognize it as her moment, and live her moment, with the insight that everybody has to come from somewhere.

Inclusivity's social experiment began to have a profoundly positive affect on Carmel and everyone around her. She began touching lives with her mere passion for the experiment. The more lives she touched, the more passionate she became. She could feel it. It was surreal. How did she end up here? So far from torte and cartoons.

Word about the experiment had spread back to Northern California. Even Jack, the fisherman from Fort Bragg, had heard about it! Amir, at the Dollar Tree store in Novato could not stop talking about the rainy Sunday morning he met her, when she made a mad dash into his store for some paper and a pen. He gave her a Hershey's chocolate kiss and his pen. He told her, "Keep on writing! Don't stop!"

Inclusivity had helped Carmel find herself again. Her authentic self. The one the world needed just as much as she did.

While walking surfside with Olga's two neighbors one afternoon, along a nice stretch of beach near the Ritz-Carlton, Laguna Niguel, Inclusivity could not believe it had already been three weeks.

She thought about her exciting friend, Nasime, in guest relations at the coastal resort, whom she met when she splurged on a couple of nights there. Nasime offered her a glass of champs directly upon her arrival. She gave her a gift bag with a bath bomb and a frame to frame a new adventure.

Before leaving the O.C., Inclusivity extended an invitation to all the millennial friends she had made, to come visit her in San Francisco. She offered them her vacant garden studio as accommodation, free of charge.

The garden studio was located below her two full floor flats, on street level. It had easy access to public transportation and was a short distance to the sophisticated shops, restaurants, and high-end eateries of Chestnut Street. It was very near the recreation parks and open spaces that were Crissy Field, The Marina Green, The Palace of Fine Arts and Fort Mason.

Angaura and the millennials would love that playground. His search engine did not lack links. Transbay Transit Center and Salesforce Park in SoMa would definitely rev their engines.

Inclusivity had grown very fond of Marissa Marie. They had experienced generational cohesion while opening a package of Krazy Glue. They were gluing sequins to the papier-mache 2020 numbers for Ainsley's New Year's Eve Party that last evening in Orange County.

The onshore winds began to pick up and they quickly high-stepped it away from the surf. It was high tide when Inclusivity's phone alerted with a new message. It was a picture of her grandson, Adam, on a boogie board.

It was an even higher tide when her phone alerted with a second message. It was a picture from Louisa. A picture of Louisa and Carmel on Carmel's wedding day.

Inclusivity realized that losing her relationship with her sister, over an unfiltered comment about prosciutto, was childish and petty. It didn't matter what the results were from something she sent off in an envelope. They would always be sisters.

Inclusivity wasted no time. She called Louisa and wished her sister a "Happy New Year!" They made a plan to meet at the Top of the Mark, to toast the Leap year and their unbreakable bond.

That New Year's Eve, Inclusivity and inclusion were in

top form. It was a cozy dinner and discussion that ended with a game of Cornhole and a view of fireworks over the bluffs. And Smores', Inclusivity's favorite dessert, at the firepit.

A neighbor named Sally did a double-handed Happy New Year wave from her balcony. Sally worked at the post office.

Pablo, A Gen Z friend of Ainsley's whom she met at Ohana Fest, stood up from his place at the table early in the evening. He gave a celebratory *wish* to the group and a word of *thanks* to the hosts. He had to leave. He was going to see his mother. It didn't matter what party he was at on New Year's Eve. Every year, it was the same thing. He said, "That woman put herself through hell for me! I love my mother."

Inclusivity hollered, "WooHoo!" and then looked around. She couldn't believe the strong sense of self that had sprung forth from her. Maybe it was the promise of the New Year. Maybe it was the "Controlla" in her. Maybe, it was Carmel rising.

When Ainsley's fathers brought the main course to the table and set it down, the experiment had come full circle. Ainsley's fathers cooked a ham.

# HOMELAND GENERATION (GEN Z); NEVADA & CHICHI

Nevada and ChiChi, pronounced "CheeChee", are sisters. They are smart, well-mannered, and have chubby cheeks that solicit cute aggression.

Their mother is Stephanie. Stephanie is my millennial positivity coach. Stephanie coaches everyone from stay-at-home-moms starting their own businesses to executives and CEO's. She really is quite good. Her specialty is explaining the importance of life/work balance to all generations through guided example.

Stephanie once changed the thoughts of a Gen X senior vice president at a multinational retail corporation who discouraged his millennial employees from listening to music on their iPods during work breaks. Stephanie made the VP close his eyes, sit quietly and listen to "Footloose" by Kenny Loggins on repeat for forty-five minutes. When the VP was done, he ripped out his earbuds, thanked Stephanie profusely and said he couldn't wait to get back to work.

Stephanie is always reminding me that staying positive is the key, no matter what door you're trying to open. She is weight bearing. She gives sympathy, offers support and encouragement; promotes self-care, sheet masks, and the three-minute meditations of the Calm app.

Stephanie's husband, Massimo, is a handsome and cool millennial from Rome. That's where they met. Stephanie felt positive about a life with Massimo when he opened the door of his Uber van and gave her an authentic tour of Rome. She discovered they had similar interests and enjoyed his company immensely. They snacked on vegetarian suppli from a street food vendor and saw a matinee screening of *Cinema Paradiso* at Nuovo Sacher, a cult status cinema in the hip and happening neighborhood of Trastevere.

Aside from occasionally driving for a safe taxi service, no one really knew what Massimo did for a living. Massimo referred to himself as a dealmaker, whatever that meant. Younger adults accepted the title. Some were even impressed with it. Older adults thought of Monty Hall.

Stephanie didn't care what people thought of their relationship. It worked for them. She found Massimo's unconventional approach to life refreshing, even exciting.

Stephanie and Massimo were married in a convention

center with 800 guests and an invitation that recommended you eat before you get there. Stephanie was well connected and had become friends with many of her clients. They had a blessed life. No complaints.

Nevada complained at her Great Grandmother's house that night, during a sleepover, that she didn't like her name. It had been grandparent's day at Nevada's daycare that day and the Great Grandmother was exhausted.

She looked at Daisy, Nevada's Puli puppy, chewing a crunchy doggie bagel on her good rug. The Great Grandmother surrendered to the thought that at least Daisy wasn't chewing the rug itself. Her house had become a human-canine daycare.

Daisy was entitled. Her dogwalker let her walk on either side of her handler.

The Great Grandmother and Nevada had gone on a color hunt earlier in the day. After finishing the hunt, the Great Grandmother's feet were so sore, she sat down in the classroom and took off her shoes. Nevada saw the Great Grandmother's inflamed joint at the base of her great toe, jumped up and down and screamed, "Pink!" It was the one color no one had been able to find. They won a trophy.

The Great Grandmother picked dry Playdough spaghetti out of her recently styled hair and tried to focus on what Nevada was saying. It was taking Nevada a long time to say it.

She contemplated looking in the puppy's overnight bag. Stephanie told her that just in case the puppy showed signs of anxiety, she had packed a bottle of human CBD oil. The Great Grandmother thought of rubbing the oil into the tops and bottoms of her feet. Nevada pulled at the one-piece house dress the Great Grandmother was wearing, abruptly recovering her from the thought.

Nevada wanted to have a shorter name like her older sister ChiChi. Her daycare teacher said she could have one. Teacher was always telling the class they had choices. Nevada was three.

That night, the Great Grandmother found herself with a choice to make of her own. Should she or should she not give her great granddaughter a nickname?

She had a fear of losing great granddaughter opportunities. After all, these were Stephanie's kids. The Great Grandmother caught a break when she remembered that Stephanie's mission in life was to always stay positive.

On a phone call the next morning with ChiChi, Stephanie's banjolele playing Mini-Me at six years old, the Great Grandmother confided in ChiChi her secret. For Nevada's birthday, she was contemplating giving Nevada a nickname. That is, if she could think of one. Enthusiastically, and with all the positivity she could quietly muster, ChiChi whispered, "Try it! Just try it!" Then she told her great grandmother not to lay on the floor, there were germs there.

Risking fallout from the entitlement missile that her Silent Generation friends might launch and inspired by the words of a Mini-Me, Nevada's great grandmother took a stand and let Nevada have her way. She entitled her to a nickname.

Apparently entitling a three-year old is not that easy. The Great Grandmother wanted the experience but would wait until Nevada went home.

Nevada's au pair showed up right on time and picked up Nevada. Stephanie sent a pet car transport service to pick up Daisy and bring her to her veterinary acupuncture appointment.

The Great Grandmother pushed past procrastination and approached her dining room table.

She had a positive attitude, a bullet journal that Stephanie gave her, and a complimentary pen from her plumber. She sat down at her table with a cup of instant coffee and a cinnamon pull-apart from Scandia Bakery. The Great Grandmother began pulling that task apart.

She concentrated, her train of thought not making any stops. She handwrote a name and crossed it out. She doodled for inspiration. She stared across the room at a fort, made with the cushions of her sofa.

A passenger called Distraction, had jumped on her train.

The Great Grandmother looked around the table at a sloppy stack of paper bills, a *Harry Potter* novel, and a high blood pressure monitor that her friend, Laura, gave her. Laura's high blood pressure was cruising at beautifully balanced lows and she didn't need it anymore.

The Great Grandmother's mood was dropping. She began to feel depressed. Maybe this whole thing was a bad idea.

She picked up the iPhone that her daughter, Rita, Stephanie's mother, did not think she could manage and managed it. The Great Grandmother went into her favorites and confidently tapped the name Rita. She got Rite Aid. Eventually, she got her glasses and got Rita.

"Hello?" Rita said.

"Hi, I'm so frustrated," the Great Grandmother said, "I tried calling you twice and I kept getting Rite Aid."

"I told you! You should have kept your flip phone. Go see Carlos at Verizon."

"What is the word for that online encyclopedia? I want to

look something up and I can't remember the name," the Great Grandmother asked.

"I don't know," Rita answered, in a curt tone.

"The name of the online encyclopedia."

"I heard you. I don't know."

"Yes, you do!" the Great Grandmother said, confident Rita had all the answers.

"Mom, I have to go."

"Is it Spanakopita?!"

Rita hung up on the Great Grandmother with a great deal of Baby Boomer annoyance. She was doing her taxes.

Rita's perennial negative attitude was not so perennial. It was actually evergreen. It had been the impetus for her daughter, Stephanie, becoming a positivity coach.

The Great Grandmother struggled silently with her first world problem while playing Mahjong in the suburbs that afternoon. After all, her name was Julia. Massimo and Stephanie had created the great grandmother name Joy. What would Nevada's nickname be?

Doubt crept in like the creeper it is and scared Joy. What if the nickname Joy chose was, WRONG.

This was too much. Joy grabbed those real bone Mahjong tiles that secretly made her feel bad due to latent onset awareness about animal cruelty and decided that if she was going to risk the entitlement conversation with her friends at all, she might as well go big.

A prideful and progressive entitler, Joy let Nevada choose the nickname herself.

The outcome was not good.

Nevada's fourth birthday party was a unicorn party. Massimo had suggested a full venue buyout at Topgolf, but it was already bought out. They compromised with a food truck and the parallel experience of a putting green in their private, retreat-like backyard.

The pastel food truck had a gold unicorn horn on the hood and winged awnings over the pass-through windows. They served unicorn ice cream rolls, rainbow grilled cheese, kale chips, and pixie dust popped sorghum. Joy actually liked sorghum because it was virtually hulless and didn't stick in her teeth. No cheese could compare to a wedge of Monterey Jack from Vella Cheese, the first solar powered company in Sonoma. That renewed Joy's energy just thinking about it.

Joy took Nevada's hand. In front of a beaming ChiChi in a unicorn headband and all of their loved ones, they had the nickname reveal. Never was there such pause at a four-year old's party.

Nevada jumped for Joy! Nevada was more excited in the arms of her great grandmother, with her new nickname, than about any of the wrapped gifts on the table.

Their love became infectious. Nevada's birthday celebration and the number 4 birthday candle on her Kara's Cupcake, were lit. It was a light that could not be extinguished.

ChiChi played a winning six-year old version of "Happy Birthday" on the banjolele.

It was the happiest birthday celebration in the history of recorded birthday celebrations. It was LOUD. LOUDER than the ring tone on Joy's iPhone.

It was almost as much fun as an event at La Luz!

The millennials were happy, Gen Z was happy, Jay-Z was happy, Gen X, baby boomers, the Silent Generation, and every single member of our championship Golden State Warriors were making some noise! Only not when it came to

Joy. No one was speaking to her. Exclusion had crashed the party.

Although most of the partygoers realized that Joy had given Nevada the best gift and freedom of all, there were those who could not get past the nickname.

Nevada had apparently spent some time around her daycare teacher's toddler. She chose the nickname Dada.

In a rare family moment, someone handed Joy a Fernet-Branca cocktail. It was that person's attempt at being the stand-out inclusive.

Joy took the biggest sip of her life and said the words, "Screw it."

With that, Joy crossed over a generational line that she didn't even know she'd been behind. She was woke and screamed out, "If Nevada's happy being Dada, let her be Dada!"

Joy was becoming inebriated and emotional. She swatted at a quadcopter flying over her head. Her tower of self-esteem was tilting and sinking.

Joy felt she couldn't even entitle her great grandchild properly. She supposed it was ALL her fault, even the fact Rita was a helicopter parent to Stephanie. It's a wonder Stephanie got away from that helicopter and escaped the airport at all.

A thirsty cousin with a goal to be Instagram famous, leaned in with his iPad to take a selfie and create some insta-Joy. He kissed Joy on the head and told her not to be salty. He told her she might be more liked than the photo of an egg. "Joy 4L!" he screamed.

"What the hell was that supposed to mean?!" Joy thought to herself as she touched the hair on top of her head and took another sip.

Fernet-Branca was good now. Back in the day, Joy took it when she had an upset stomach. Pairing Fernet with the sweetness of cider had made Joy feel, joyful.

Joy chased the lemon wheel garnish around her glass with that pitiful rosemary stem and ate a gluten free brownie so heavy, she could hardly lift it. She wondered why she hadn't just stayed home and ordered Take-out from Dehli Belly like Stephanie and Massimo always did. Or better yet, taken a trip to The City and grabbed a solo spot at the Swan Oyster Depot.

Instead, Joy sat with liquid remorse and Dada's doula, engaged in a conversation about how Joy once gave a tablespoon of Fernet to Rita when she was eleven, to help her sleep. If Joy ever gave a tablespoon of Fernet to an eleven-year old Dada, Joy was positive, the positivity, would drain right out of Stephanie.

The doula excused herself. She was leaving to enjoy some Johnny Cash songs and the live music of Train Wreck Junction at The Reel. Joy's train wreck was far too real.

Massimo must have made the cocktail. At least he was good for something. Joy never liked him. She thought Stephanie deserved better, but she respected the fine line between wanting to get involved and knowing when to stay out of it.

Massimo spent too much time playing ping-pong at the couple's social club, making small bets, and hanging with his surfer friends on Maverick's Beach in Half Moon Bay. Why did he wear a beanie on the top of his head? What was he trying to prove?

Massimo was too much work for Joy. She didn't have the bandwidth. She would have to take her growing concern to her social club, otherwise known as the 11 A.M. Sunday mass at St. Francis with Father Alvin.

In Joy's mind, Massimo was a Mr. Smarty Pants. His sense of humor escaped her.

Massimo stood across the room holding Nevada, tapping his foot in the Gucci Horsebit mule that Stephanie bought him at Barney's. He chuckled as he looked at Joy and mouthed the words, "Dada".

"And that's what I'm talking about!" Joy said to herself, as she finished her drink and set down the empty glass with a bit of Fernet force.

She remembered how Massimo laughed when he pulled the Jimmy Kimmel Halloween Candy Prank and videotaped Nevada while pretending to steal her Halloween candy. Joy wondered how Massimo would react if someone pulled a Millennial Ping-Pong Prank and videotaped him while pretending to steal his ping- pong balls.

Massimo knew he had mouthed off as much as he could. After all, Joy knew the secret. The secret behind the name Nevada. Nevada was conceived the night Stephanie and Massimo won big at skill-based gaming in Vegas.

Sunday could not come fast enough. It was the one day out of the week, Joy found peace.

My mother is good friends with Joy. Most every Sunday after mass, they venture over to Napa to do a bit of shopping. Typically, they end up at the tables in the Genova Delicatessen.

That Sunday, Joy nursed a Fernet hangover and bought herself a BLT taco. Although she wasn't exactly sure what she was eating or if she could even eat it, there was one thing Joy was certain of. She was entitled.

# LIFE CAN BE TOUGH,
# FOR A GEN Z GIRL

Life can be tough for a Gen Z girl. But, before you go off Googling or wondering what a Gen Z girl is like, let me stop you. It doesn't really matter. All you need to know is, she's a girl.

As a girl, when life got tough and I needed perspective, there was always my favorite doll. Laffing Sal.

Laffing Sal was an animatronic doll who stood approximately six feet tall on a platform all her own. She had bouncy curls, a missing front tooth, freckles, vibrant fuchsia colored cheeks and was encased in a humongous glass box. Not only was she amusing, but she never failed to brighten your spirits.

Laffing Sal used to be located in the Musee Mechanique at the Cliff House.

Laffing Sal and a Pronto Pup, on the headland above the cliffs, was a casual fun afternoon. You put your coin in the slot and Laffing Sal, laughed hysterically.

Throughout my life, I would visit Laffing Sal. I brought my father to see her later in his life when he had failing health and was a tough audience for Sal.

Sal still got him.

A dad-daughter relationship, once cultivated, is a perfect 10.

When my good Gen X friend, Annamaria C, heard I was writing something multigenerational, she told me about her Gen Z teenage daughter's inability to speak to her Gen X father. The parents are divorced. When real life issues arise, and the daughter is with her father, she feels she cannot discuss certain topics with him. The father does not know how to communicate, and the daughter does not understand where he's coming from.

The following story is a little dad-daughter reduction for a Gen Z girl.

This story is inspired by true events.

It was a below zero, bitterly cold and overcast December day, in my mother's hometown of St. Paul, Minnesota. Based on the new formula, the Wind Chill Factor was 40 degrees below zero.

My traditional family left the 65 degree weather and our home on Darien Way in San Francisco, to fly to St. Paul for Christmas.

My traditional family consisted of my Silent father and Silent mother, my Gen X brother and Gen X me. I was eleven years old.

We would stay with my great-aunt Flora. She was the Greatest Generation. Truly, she was marvelous. Aunt Flora lived to be 106 years old. She had me take her to The Lex for Walleye Cakes when she was 105.

From the time I was very little, I was always surrounded by older people. I used to stay with my grandmother on Cobb Mountain during summer vacations. We had a black and white television that received one channel, Channel 3, and it was blurry. It came into focus three times a day: "The Phil Donahue Show" in the late afternoon, "Little House on the Prairie" at prime time, and the local news and weather followed by "The Tonight Show" with Johnny Carson in the late evening. If you wanted to know if it was going to rain the next day, you had to stay up until 11:30 P.M.

Today's Gen Zer, I am convinced, would lose their collectively cool and tech-savvy mind if they took a trip in that time machine.

Back on that December day, forty-two years ago, we arrived at MSP Airport. My mother had a big family and several family members were waiting for us at the gate. There was a big turnout because my mother had not been back for a Christmas with the fam in Minnesota since, the exodus.

The exodus was when my risk-taking mother, along with four twentysomething registered nurses in her social group, had all taken leaves of absence or quit their jobs.

All of the young women and their parents met up for a Bratwurst and Egg breakfast in Stillwater. It was the perfect kickstart to their early morning departure. After breakfast, the young women hugged their parents, jumped in three cars, and drove cross country to California. The year was 1961.

They drove off in the dead of winter. The logic of youth was alive and well.

Years later, my father would joke that it was a marriage

caravan. Never under estimate the intelligence of a marriage caravan, caravanning down the highway in 1961.

My mother's car was a two-tone green 1953 Buick Dynaflow Transmission.

Up until that time, the only risk my mother had taken, was answering a call in the rectory of Saint Agnes Church one Sunday and putting it on hold. Her uncle, Father Kevin, was a Catholic priest.

The relatives all remembered my mother's spunky spirit, which she never lost. They thought it might be funny to re-enact the exodus a week after our arrival and caravan to a hypermarket for some holiday shopping. There was no Mall of America at that time. Twenty family members entered the store together.

I entered the store with a stomach cramp.

Aunt Flora took me by the hand and called upon distraction when she pointed out a Gold Medal Skier Barbie on the shelf. She told me I could win a gold medal if I wanted to. "You might just have to have her," Aunt Flora would say.

This was a celebratory trip after all, and Aunt Flora saw nothing wrong with spoiling yourself just a little bit.

When it came to showing class, Aunt Flora was a heavyweight. All 85 pounds of her. The heaviest thing on Aunt Flora, were the three 18 karat gold bangles that rolled around clanking into each other on her thin wrist.

Distraction uncooperative and craving the one thing Aunt Flora believed was keeping her alive, she headed off to the chip aisle for a bag of Cheetos.

My mother and I headed off to the restroom.

No matter what generation you're in, where you are when

you get your period for the first time, is something you'll always remember.

My mother helped me feel my feelings that day. She was kind and re-told me the story about the night I was born.

It is the miracle of life and for most, a private moment.

I remember I felt faint and light headed. I remember the SOUND. The SOUND of the floor intercom:

**WILL ALL MEMBERS OF THE SCHMIDT FAMILY PLEASE COME TO THE FRONT OF THE STORE**

The Gold Medal Skier Barbie stood poised on the dresser in Aunt Flora's guest room where I had landed. I could hear a much better sound, the sound of my Uncle Izzy making me one of his famous chocolate milkshakes. Add some White Castle sliders and that was entitlement in 1976.

I became ill, actually, and Uncle Izzy's brother, Dr. Roy from Edina, recommended I stay in bed for a couple of days. Now, not only did I not feel well, I felt terrible. I had ruined the celebration.

Oddly, it didn't tum out that way.

My family decided to pay me a visit. All twenty of them. They had hyped out of that hypermarket and headed straight for Aunt Flora's.

Aunt Flora didn't have children. As a result, they were all her children. That's the way it was.

There is an old school rule that when a person is sick, you visit them and bring them a gift. My father puffed extra hard on his pipe that day, as he walked upstairs to visit me, carrying his gifts.

My father, at his own personal request, had been sleeping downstairs in Aunt Flora's basement home office with full bath and Mid-Century Daybed. He loved the privacy, loved watching broadcast golf and football, and enjoyed perusing the law books.

My father and Uncle Izzy were attorneys.

In the basement of Aunt Flora's house, my father could escape the sound of the Yaks.

Yaks by definition are family members who haven't seen each other in several years and have to catch up.

These weren't domestic Yaks. These were wildly wonderful Cheeto feeding Yaks.

The sweet smell of my father's favorite Jim Mate tobacco wafted up the stairs ahead of him and into the room.

I remember having a definite opinion about not wanting to see him that day. It was just too embarrassing. I felt awkward and uneasy. The kind of uneasiness that comes with an unanswered text.

What could he possibly say?

There he was. There we were. Dad- daughter.

My father stood at the end of the bed and said, "I understand you're a woman now."

Die.

Hide.

Die.

Hide.

I was horrified. How could my father, the ultimate wordsmith, who was a regular contributor to Herb Caen's column and who enjoyed reading the dictionary as if it were a novel, choose those wrong words for me?

My father spoke his words confidently. He had actually

spent a lot of time on them. He felt comfortable saying those words. He said them with pride and the good feeling of conviction that comes with appropriateness.

I realized years later, that my father's words were brilliant that day. He had given me the ultimate gift. One word. Respect.

His second gift, not so much. He reached under his arm and pulled out a board game of Scrabble.

My poor father, I thought to myself. He must have been as confused about all of this as I was.

My father wasn't confused. The board game was my father's way of extending an invitation to play many fun games of Scrabble together, for the love of words.

Finally, there was his last gift. This one, was not to be believed.

My father handed me a plush racoon toy. It had a tail that was coarse and lifelike. It had big, cold plastic eyes. And felt talons.

I remember thinking, "Is this all the store had? What about a Teddy Bear?"

There were no hypermarkets in San Francisco in 1976. I actually wrote a creative short story while I was in bed about a girl who only got her period in Minnesota.

My father looked at the raccoon and then at me, waiting for me to say something.

"Thank you," I said.

Secretly, I wanted to cry. Not because I was sad. Not because I was mad. But, because I was touched.

My father, although we had our disagreements now and then, was my soulmate.

He always told me, "Take your turn. You'll have your chance. Go for the brass ring! Never give up!" He always had my back.

He taught me that no self is perfect. Life is not perfect. To learn how to get the job done with some of the pieces missing. Learn how to forgive yourself when you fall short. "To think only the best, to work for the best, and expect only the best." My father was an Optimist. He was the Optimist International Governor of District CAL-U-NEV. That is a quote from The Optimist Creed.

For all of his wisdom, my dad had not known what to do that day. But, he understood the basic principle of effort. To do nothing, would have been negligent. He would have let down a little girl. His little girl. Who thought her father was everything. He *was* GOAT.

Morals of the story: As long as someone is doing the best they can, that's all that matters. The only way to start a conversation is just to begin. And never, ever give a girl having her period for the first time, a plush raccoon toy. Unless, it's the best you can do.

I did my best at consoling Aunt Flora the day we left. I remember she cried an atmospheric river. Her neighbor, Ana Paula, who had been away studying Art History at Fordham University, would be over shortly to visit. She would bring with her, her younger brother, David. They would all sit around the little table near Aunt Flora's kitchen window, watching Ruby red cardinals eat from a snow-covered bird feeder hanging on a bare tree.

David would help Aunt Flora's nephew, Gene, shovel the driveway.

Aunt Flora was a skilled driver in the Minnesota winters. She was still driving into her nineties, better than I could ever drive on ice. Who knew when I would see her again? She was getting older. She was 72.

On the plane ride home, I thought of my Uncle Izzy's milkshakes and my Gold Medal Skier Barbie from Aunt Flora. I thought about my mother's kindness and my father's racoon, who peered out at me from inside my backpack, on the floor under the seat ahead.

I realized I would just have to find a way to talk about it. A way to deal with it. Deal with this inescapable reality, this coming of age houseguest, who would visit me almost every single month without fail, for the next thirty-six years.

I named my period, Gloria.

# IF YOU MAKE A MESS, CLEAN IT UP! - NEPOTISM AT THE ZOO

**This is a story about the Kalama Zoo in Michigan.**

The zebras were fine, their stripes were aligned.
The pandas chewed stems of bamboo;
The tigers growled louder than you before coffee,
What broke out in Kalama Zoo?
It wasn't truism, and that's no lie.
Sensationalism would be no distortion;
There was **NEPOTISM** in Kalama Zoo,
and each section had their portion.
Take the tuna crab exhibit, for example,
The man hired there didn't know;
anything about tuna crab really,
he was just dating Zoo Keeper, Flo.
Her son, Gary, was sound checking canaries,
The hyenas forgot how to laugh;
Kalama Zoo, had social animal issues,
when a snow leopard catfished a giraffe.

A lot of good help showed up at the zoo,
they were turned away and instead;
friends and family got hired in all the positions,
and management turned her head.
The Brown Twins did not visit the zoo anymore,
a circus is more what it was;
when Flo's cousin rode by on a hippo,
it was more than the local buzz.
Photogs with cameras showed up at the zoo,
white vans with big satellite dishes;
Flo deliberately made a big mess of things,
because life had not granted her wishes.
Flo's generation would be my creation,
Kalama Zoo is pure make believe;
If you make a mess, clean it up!
A message for all to receive.

## ▼

# MILLENNIALS (GEN Y); SOFIA & MIGUEL

Sofia and Miguel are young millennial doctors, married to each other. They are beguiled and in love. Miguel is my cousin's son. I spent Thanksgiving with them and the rest of the family in Mill Valley, at a townhome with a breathtaking view of Mt. Tam.

On our way, we stopped at Whole Foods for a loaf of Della Fattoria's signature Meyer Lemon and Rosemary bread. That loaf of bread alone, was something to be thankful for.

A millennial cashier wearing a grey hoodie beneath a black cotton apron, marked with the name Pedro, motioned me over to his line. "Hi, how are you?" he asked.

"Happy Thanksgiving," I said.

"Happy Thanksgiving!"

As he scanned the loaf of bread, I inserted my chipped debit card to pay and said, "I'm writing a book."

"Congrats! What's it about?"

"It's about the millennials."

"I just wrote a paper about the millennials."

"Really? How'd that go?"

"I got an A. But, that's just because the teacher didn't know anything about what it's like to be a millennial."

"What is it like to be a millennial?"

A woman behind me coughed in my ear, to let me know to speed it up.

"In one word," I said.

"Stressful," Pedro said.

I paid for my bread and started towards the door. Pedro hollered and jogged after me with my debit card.

"Thank you! Thank you!" I said. "I think I'm going to give you a cameo in my book."

"I'll link it to my page!" Pedro exclaimed.

"You'll do what?"

"I don't have one yet, but maybe I will one day."

"Have one, what? What do you mean your page?"

"If I'm ever relevant enough to be in Wikipedia, I'll link your book to my Wikipedia page."

I understood right then what he meant by stressful. Being a millennial, with a generational goal to change the world, is an innate pressure.

Some millennials shared with me, that they feel they are competing with themselves. Trying to prove to themselves, their families and their peers, that they can do things. That they are good at something. They feel pressured by having to overcome the disbelief and the skepticism.

"Pedro," I said.

"Yeah?" Pedro responded.

"You're already relevant."

"Thanks," Pedro said, as he gave a little wave and hurried back to his register.

I had better hurry myself, or I would be late for dinner.

There is nothing like a great soup to unite the generations. I was expecting tortellini from Della Santina's, but this year my cousin made her amazing butternut squash soup. Family members request it periodically throughout the year, it's that good. She explained the secret; buying real butternut squash and taking the time to peel them herself. The butternut squash already peeled at the store, just aren't the same.

I have great admiration for my cousin, Lisa. She is an altruistic person. She understands that the love is in the details. She always starts her proper table with a beautiful tablecloth from Coquelicot in Larkspur.

I appreciated her efforts. It was an honor to be invited to her table.

The first course of soup, in the Williams Sonoma pumpkin bowls, did not disappoint.

My place card was to the left of Sofia, since she put them out and we hadn't had a chance to catch up in a while. Miguel was seated next to her, on her right-hand side.

As I went to sit down, I noticed a place card with the name *Sheala* written in calligraphy. I asked Sofia, "Who is Sheala?"

"Her name's pronounced Shay-la. She's just a really good friend. I never get to see her except when we're both home. She'll be here in a little bit," Sofia said, "Best future lawyer in the state of Idaho."

"Nice," I said, thinking of the future and reassured the millennials have it covered.

Sofia said she forgave me for not attending their beach wedding in Puerto Rico in 2016. I couldn't remember my reason and she was quick to remind me it was Zika.

I felt sorry that I had missed their wedding over a mosquito.

I was so happy Miguel had sealed the deal with Sofia. For the longest time she was known as "Not my girlfriend".

Sofia thanked me for the comforter that I brought them for their new apartment. A comforter in the correct size is the secret to a good night's sleep.

Sofia is a beautiful woman and Puerto Rican proud. She keeps it real. I find her candor refreshing. She tells it like it is.

My mother, seated at the head of the table, told Sofia and Miguel how Thanksgiving used to be her holiday. How she used to bake all of her own pies from scratch and stand on a step stool, single-handedly mashing potatoes for twenty-five guests.

The Silent Generation chef in my mother, suddenly overwhelmed by the stark realization that she was no longer the potato masher, made a mad dash for thankfulness and changed the subject. She was completely well-intentioned when she asked Sofia and Miguel if they planned to have children.

"We have to have our honeymoon first," Sofia answered.

It had been almost three years since Sofia and Miguel were married and they still had not had a honeymoon. They were exhausted, butt busting millennials with busy schedules. They were putting themselves through medical school and doing a great job concealing the dark circles of student loan debt that encircled them.

There was one thing that made it all worth it. They were living their bliss.

Miguel spoke about existing on a diet of tuna fish and peas, which he defended because it gave him his protein.

I was impressed by their work ethic, unwavering devotion and personal sacrifice, yet equally aware of my mother's pending curiosity about children.

"Maybe you'll have twins," I said to Miguel.

"Miguel says if we have twins, that's it for him!" Sofia said.

A confident and quick-witted Miguel agreed. "Same day," he said, "I don't want to pay for parking twice."

I thought how difficult it must be to raise kids in today's world. I brought up the news I had seen on television that morning, about a university in the U.K. no longer using red ink to grade papers, because the students perceived it as mean. Green, was apparently the new red.

Miguel sat up and enunciated, "I grade all of my university students' papers in red. It's the correcting color. I learned that at St. Francis."

I was enthralled. The bells had tolled. The millennial myth was turning into understanding before my very eyes. Millennials could not be stereotyped. They wouldn't stand for it. Each one had their story.

I shared privately with Sofia that I had started writing again and briefly touched on the topic. She was excited for me and my new project. She gave me a Hopper's Hands high-five.

I was surprised by and thankful for her support, but then this was Sofia. Not everyone was like her.

My project was risky, but passion denied me surrender. I had to push myself. Risk the conversation. The bright-eyed millennial Sofia helped me get it started. She sat sideways in her chair and said, "Ask me."

I looked at her and I asked, "What can you tell me about millennials? What should I know?"

Sofia told me the basic millennial message is just to lead with respect and love.

She added that she'd been raised around a lot of older people, so that's why she understood me. I received it as a compliment.

Sofia made a point to say that she always listens to both sides of everything and then makes her decision. There are always two sides to every argument.

Across the table, a Gen X mother named Lynn and her Gen Z teenage daughter named Linnea, were in disagreement. Linnea was dressed in a panda onesie and anxiously awaiting the hour of midnight when it would officially be Black Friday.

House rules allowed for no one to ditch the fruitful family dinner before then.

The millennials would opt for online shopping, coupon codes and instant shipping, but the Gen Z consumer was a different animal.

Lynn and Linnea had been a dynamic mother-daughter duo all day, but the retail troop of two was growing weary. They could have used the reinforcements of Girl Scout Troop #10117!

Lynn and Linnea disagreed over where they were, exactly,

when the Costco pie slid across the back seat of the car and lodged in the door jamb, earlier that afternoon.

"We were in the parking lot at Costco," Lynn said.

"It was Home Depot."

"It was Costco."

"It was Home Depot."

"It was Costco!"

"It was Home Depot!"

"MOM! We stopped in the parking lot at Costco. Don't you remember?!"

"Linnea, when I pulled over, we had already left Costco. We were in the Home Depot parking lot."

Lynn glanced over at me for some Gen X support, frustrated by the tenacity and absurdity of the disagreement and somewhat mortified it had found its way to our dinner table. She stared at Linnea, wondering if they should share. "Should we tell them, Linnea?"

Linnea ignored her mother and began applying nail polish stickers to the nails of the hostess.

Lynn leaned in and calmly said, "We bought an apple pie at Costco this afternoon. They're huge."

"Oh, I know. They're so good. We bought a pumpkin pie there last week. I could eat the whole thing myself with a fork and a cup of coffee."

"Well, as we were driving, the pie was on the back seat and we watched it slide towards the side of the door. You know, they're in those really big plastic containers."

Linnea interjected, "We were at Costco!"

"Linnea, it was Home Depot."

"Mom, we were not!! There is no Home Depot at that shopping center. WE WERE AT COSTCO!"

I had to rescue this poor woman. Gen Z had her pinned. She was relentless.

I asked Lynn, "Is there a Home Depot in Novato?"

"No. In San Rafael. It was the Home Depot in San Rafael. We went to Costco and then as we were driving home, I pulled off the highway into the parking lot of Home Depot."

Linnea stopped midway through her sticker application. She realized she had gone too far and pushed her mother to the point of self-fact-checking.

It was on that rainy Thanksgiving night in Mill Valley that a Gen Z girl had a consideration to make of her own; maybe her mother was right.

Linnea welcomed the thought in for a moment, then shook her panda head and began texting. She wanted to know what time her friends and her friend's mother were picking her up and taking her to a brick-and-mortar Nordstrom.

Her bubbly personality quickly turned the conversation to laughter and the sharing of memes.

I was shocked to overhear that her two best friends, sixteen and seventeen years old, who had grown up in Mill Valley, had never been to San Francisco.

Mill Valley is approximately 21 minutes to San Francisco by car with no traffic. If you take the ferry from nearby Sausalito to the historic SF Ferry Building, now a bustling urban marketplace, it's approximately 30 minutes. Those extra nine minutes are well spent on the experience. The girls had never had the experience at all.

Having been born on Valentine's Day, the romantic in me felt for their isolation in not climbing to their star on a little cable car. The pragmatist in me understood there were stars in Mill Valley, too.

Who would have known that Valentine's Day would miss out in 2019 with the selling of NECCO, the oldest confectionery company in the United States, that typically produced 8-billion of those tiny conversation Sweethearts a year. Spangler Company would issue a sweet statement to their fans: "Miss U 2," "Wait 4 Me," and "Back Soon."

Sofia and Miguel would leave soon. They would be lodging at nearby Cavallo Point, compliments of baby boomer parents. The family ski trip to Heavenly had a meet up time of 7 A.M. in the parking lot of the Cheesecake Factory. It was the next best thing to skiing the Dolomites.

A mobile phone vibrated in a wireless charger on a nearby marble counter top.

The hostess, somewhat rattled by all of the chaos and definitely perplexed at her half-done nails, searched for the bottle of champagne she had purchased especially for the occasion. She picked up the conversation and asked what we were all dying to know, "So, what happened to the pie?!"

An exhausted Lynn replied, "We couldn't save it. Then the seagulls came."

The hostess laughed and asked, "The seagulls got the pie?"

"Well, Linnea was able to grab part of it. We brought it home to Elliott."

Lynn looked down the table at her teenage son sitting quietly next to his father and uncle. He was a ballplayer, nearly six feet tall. Relieved by the mere face of her mellow Elliott, Lynn continued, "Elliott didn't care what it looked like. He'll eat anything."

Sofia and I turned our heads and looked at each other. Sofia shrugged. There was no need to decide this one. It had decided itself.

## WOMANLY WISDOMS FROM THE CABOWEB:

S TRIVE

NEVER TO BE A

MANIPULATIVORA CUNNINGOSA.

T HRIVE

AS A STRONGORA WOMANOSA.

MAKE YOURSELF THE TOTALORA PACKAGEOSA.

WALK AWAY WHEN YOU MUST.

WALK THE GODDESSORA WALKOSA.

# CABOWEB

In the spirit of the millennial entrepreneur, the following is a treatment for a play I am currently writing. The working title is Caboweb.

*(The Black Widow Spider was the inspiration for the species in this play. In the play, these spiders are on stage and human sized. Their spider bodies are made of fabulous, shiny black latex. They have vivid red hourglass shapes on their undersides.)*

Once upon a time, in a land far, far away; West Hollywood to be exact, there lived a spider named Mairy. Today was Mairy's 31st birthday. The age their species marries and spins their first web. They're okay with living together for ten years, they just have a lot of other things they want to do, so they're not in any hurry to get married.

Doreen hopped into the 450 SL classic convertible car, like the grasshopper she'd just eaten, and drove in the direction of Mairy's web. It was located on the corner of Sunflower Boulevard and N Fairfax Avenue.

Doreen was Mairy's mother.

There it was, Mairy's web. The web was chic and grandiose. It was 4 bedrooms, 5 baths, complete with chef's kitchen and a rooftop patio with a killer vantage point. Gorgeous cityscape views and a hot tub rounded out the orb. Even City Hall was visible. The web was spun between the pillared stalks of two giant sunflowers.

"Brava!!!" Doreen congratulated, as she stood upright on four legs and clapped with the other four.

Mairy's claw art designs were wildly popular and had helped Mairy claw her way to the top of a fashion empire at an early age. Her latest design, a spectacled bear claw, was the standout art trend.

Doreen slinked around the locked web. Where on earth was Mairy, Doreen wondered, as she raised her dark gel manicured claw and plucked a fine stinging hair from her cheek.

She saw seven suitors struggling on the petals of the sunflowers, attempting to get free. Mairy had *tricked* them all with her alluring text messages; filled with distress, spidering talk, and time delay.

Alas, as Doreen was about to leave, she caught a glimpse of Mairy in the reflection of the glass. Doreen sneaked into Mairys web; *sneakin', sneakin', sneakin'* through an open pore. She found her out on the rooftop patio.

A vase of Little Beckas, freshly cut with sharp incisors, sat on the table.

There was Mairy, texting away. She was sunning her hourglass, listening to the Beatles, and sipping from a 1.7 oz. bottle of whiskey. Mairy was a frequent flyer.

"Mairy!" Doreen screeched, "What are you doing here? I thought you were meeting Andy for sushi in Malibu?"

"I just got home," Mairy said, "I went to the spa web in Beverly Hills for an eight-leg wax."

"Do you know you have seven suitors stuck on the breathy whispering petals of your captivating web on Sunflower Boulevard?!"

"Yep," Mairy said, applying her sunflower oil.

"What will you do with all of them, Mairy?" Doreen asked.

"Well, one of them needs to give me a ride to the airport. I'm going to Caboweb," Mairy said, checking her hourglass to see that it wasn't getting too red.

"Which one will it be, Mairy?" Doreen asked.

"I think number seven. One through five are too tired. Six has to wait for Comcast," Mairy calculated.

"I read in Forb magazine that Angela and Andy are back together," Doreen said, as she strummed the spider veins on the backs of her legs.

"Never gonna happen," Mairy said, producing a low vengeful purr, "I took care of that!"

Doreen walked over to Mairy and got in her spider space. "I don't think you ever made it to the spa web today for your eight-leg wax," Doreen said, as she took out her spectacle magnifier and examined Mairy's fifth leg, just below the fourth joint, "Oh! I see a pointed little hair right THERE!" Doreen exclaimed.

"Wow," Mairy said snidely, "You need to take your Arachnopryl."

Doreen continued, "I think, you met Andy for sushi today, and that you wrapped Andy up IN A CALIFORNIA ROLL and tucked him deep in the stalk of your web!"

"Oh, he's in there," Mairy admitted, as she bit hard into a habanero and lime antennae. Oh, Mairy didn't want Andy, but she didn't want anyone else to have him either. She just couldn't give up the ghost.

"Mairy, marry him! He's social, very subterranean," Doreen gushed.

Andy didn't even know he was in a web. If you told him, he probably wouldn't want to hear it. He was oblivious; watching a Lakers game and snacking on *guilty seeds*. He was paying a bill OVER and OVER again. A bill Mairy never paid.

If only Andy could get free of Mairy's web, his life would begin. That was a long shot. Hopefully, he'd beat the buzzer!

Doreen had gone to the country club web to work off the stress and have lunch with one of the housewives from Bravo. She was playing tennis when she heard the court phone ring. Doreen practiced her DJ inspired backspin every day. She did not appreciate the interruption and continued with her vicious drop shot.

A ball boy named William ran across the court to retrieve a stray ball. He shouted to remind Doreen that there was a call waiting. Doreen was not pleased. He made her miss, her shot. It was a BIG point.

Doreen glared at him, fixing all eight of her spider eyes on her subject. The eyes that help make the poison. Her glands became inflamed. Doreen engaged her poison control mechanism and in a tempered tone she secreted the sentence,

"I am Aware." Breaking club policy, Doreen cursed as she long legged it over to answer the court phone. It was Mairy. Doreen hung up the phone and told her friend Bhitzi, she had to spin.

Spin back over to Mairy's web.

Bhitzi bit her lip. She curled her tongue. Bhitzi's face was all out of whack. She had had botched Botox and fillers and looked like a moth. She should have just tried Kiehl's Ultra Facial Cream.

Bhitzi was pissed. She had been winning the match.

Doreen would have thanked a Higher Power for the timing, had she believed in a power higher than herself.

Clouds covered the sun and Mairy splashed in her emerald green hot tub water, foaming with envy. She was watching *Mean Girls* on her outdoor patio TV and flossing her fangs. She knew what she was. There was no denying it. She was the BEST of her species.

The door was left open for Doreen when she arrived at Mairy's web. The web was unusually quiet. A pair of novelty disguise nose glasses lay on the Large Leather luxe cowhide rug.

"Mairy!" Doreen screamed, as she crawled up the stairs to the rooftop patio, hanging onto the hemp bannister rope.

Mairy jumped out of the hot tub, did a wrap-around in her towel, and reached for her streetwear.

"What in the world is such an emergency, that you had to page me at the club?!" Doreen asked.

"There's a tick," Mairy said, softly.

"A what?"

"A tick. You know I'm afraid of ticks. Get the tick! It's

HUGE! It's on the wall!!" Mairy said, pointing to a dot on the wall.

Doreen looked at Mairy and then up at the seven suitors, now playing cricket together on the petals.

"Really?" Doreen asked, "Why didn't you text one of them to get the tick?!"

"You just do it so well," Mairy complimented.

Exasperated and as she was about to leave, Doreen asked, "Mairy, have you even checked on Andy?"

"I will," Mairy said, browsing her playlists. Mairy activated her spinneret, spritzed with some **BENGAL 88**, and spun to the stalk.

Doreen curled her legs up in a ball and began rolling; rolling back and forth on the patio, S-N-O-R-R-R-I-N-G!

Mairy launched back up to the patio and shrieked, "EEEK!!!"

"WUH, where's the tick?!" Doreen asked, as she stretched out her legs and opened her eyes, "I think I fell asleep. What is it, Mairy?"

"Andy's gone!" Mairy said in a panic.

"What do you mean Andy's gone?" Doreen asked, "Gone where?"

Angela pushed down her wings and stepped into the private Town Car waiting for her at JFK Airport. She was on her way to an event at The Strand on Broadway. Angela was an 88 butterfly. She hated making landings in busy Union Square.

Angela thought about Andy and how she had truly loved him. Once upon a time …

Her mobile phone rang. Angela looked down and

dismissed the call. She raised her tinted glass window. The Town Car pulled out and moved forward.

The BOLD WIND BLEW.

" - Wary Mairy - Wary Mairy - "

It even created a hashtag on the web. #WaryMairy

To Be Completed by the fall of 2020 …

# ▼
# BABY BUST (GEN X); MY
# GENERATION

I listed a vineyard property in Napa on the flight path of the hot air balloons.

It had panoramic views of the valley floor and four plantable acres with vineyard worthy soils so rich, there would be no need to incorporate organic matter. It had a brick pizza oven made with ancient bricks imported from the Greek city of Corinth. It also had Helen.

Helen was the Silent Generation owner who had lived on the property for over 54 years. She was on a fixed income and could no longer afford the upkeep. The house itself was older than that. It was a Silent teardown.

Helen's only marriage had been annulled. The man she had been married to was an olive grower. Forty years ago, upon discovering infestation in his fruit, Helen's husband lost his crop.

Legend in the vAlley has it, he fled the orchard with such a bitter taste in his mouth that he went to the dentist. Two weeks later he ran off with a dental hygienist who had roots in the Deep South.

Helen focused on herself and had a wonderful life. She had lots of family and friends both here and in Greece.

Helen had lots and lots of stuff. It brought back good memories. Helen had so much personal accumulation, a location scout once contacted her about featuring her out-buildings on an episode of "American Pickers".

Her latest accumulation was a Segway. Someone gave it to her as a joke, but Helen found it a very quick and convenient way to travel down the hill to her mailbox and get her mail. It was just about the only convenience she embraced in the modern world.

Trading orthotics for robotics was such fun for Helen that lately Helen had been seen bypassing the mailbox and riding through downtown Napa. She Segwayed through the Oxbow Marketplace and visitors waved from the Wine Train!

Zeus loved to chase Helen on her Segway, but he could never catch her.

Zeus was a tea cup German Shepherd. Helen had adopted Zeus years ago, when everyone said it shouldn't be done. Zeus was too young, and Helen was too old. It was a match made in Pets Lifeline. She was his ride or die.

Up until the Segway, Helen rarely left her house. She received all of her meals from DoorDash.

I was fired up when Bridgette Marmenian brought me an offer. Bridgette was the baby boomer buyer's agent. Bridgette didn't have to work. Bridgette had invented the

Bridgette Bootie that was slaying internationally and had made Bridgette a very wealthy woman.

It was an upgrade on the traditional disposable shoe cover that realtors slip over their shoes when they preview properties. Bridgette's Bootie had interactive capabilities. It was designed by one of her millennial clients.

Logan was thankfully in the deal. He loved Bridgette. Last year, Logan had also loved Bridgette's transaction coordinator, Rick. They were a millennial couple until Rick cheated with a Gen X dermatologist. Rick and the radical skin doctor had just left on a whirlwind trip to Cuba.

Logan became obsessed with the constant posts and photos on Rick's social media accounts. He was hyperconnected and hyperventilating.

Rick embraced an unrestricted lifestyle. He was tech-savvy and could remote from anywhere in the world.

Logan could emote, better than anyone else in the world. This latest post was savage. It was a photo of the intergenerational new couple in a red convertible 1955 Cadillac Eldorado. There was too much Tostones in that car. It had Logan practically draped over his steering wheel.

Rick's complexion was glowing as he stood next to his BAE. Logan's life was in the Bay-amo.

I was having my own trouble focusing on the offer Bridgette brought me. Helen bought the property in 1965 with an inheritance her mother had left her. She paid $35,000. Bridgette's offer was $4.7 million.

The property was listed at $4.4 million. Three hundred thousand dollars over the asking price was mandatory for a bragging right in the state of California.

It had been on the market for 282 days and I had only had

one showing. You could say what you want about Bridgette, but she was a strong closer.

Logan knew I was meeting Bridgette at Helen's house. Bridgette had asked if she could stop by the property and take a picture for her millennial client who was stuck in a meeting about machine learning in Santa Clara.

I knew Bridgette was using it as an excuse to meet and charm Helen as part of her Always Be Closing strategy, but I didn't care. I just needed to sell the house.

After Bridgette took the photo, Helen got up from watching a rerun of "The Bachelor" in Zermatt, placed Zeus on the floor and gave Bridgette a big hug. Helen was thrilled with her new Bridgette Booties.

I got in my car and called Logan. He answered the phone with a question, "How did it go?"

"You're not going to believe what Bridgette just said to me."

"Did she throw shade?" Logan asked.

"She walked past me on the way to her car and said, 'piece of cake'".

"That sounds like major shade. What does it even mean? A piece of cake? Why do people your age talk like that? Why can't you say your feelings?!"

"Have you eaten, Logan?"

"Yes. I just had my avocado toast. I'm not hangry."

"When do you think you'll be up here?" I asked.

"I'm still in San Francisco. This traffic is cray!" Logan said, as he drove slowly past the Painted Ladies of Postcard Row and eventually even slower through the construction and barricades of Van Ness Avenue.

Logan had just moved back to The City with his two

miniature Greyhounds, Muni and Google, that he was co-parenting with Rick. While Rick was smoking cigars and drinking mojitos, Logan's life had gone to the dogs. Thankfully, he had the Vintage Kennel Club to help him care for his starter children. As much as he complained, however, Muni and Google changed the quality of his life.

Logan was driving down Lombard Street when a GoCar, with thrill-seeking tourists navigating the city streets, cut in front of him. The tourists wore tank tops and huddled together to keep warm, while listening to a commentary on the Marina District. If this didn't move along, Logan would be tempted to call it a day and just go get a burrito in the Mission.

"The light is green! GOOOO!!!!" Logan screamed, as he blew his horn at the GoCar.

"Did you get the text I sent you that Rick called?" I asked.

"No."

"He called me on WhatsApp. Is Rick out of the country?"

"Ugh. Dying. Yes."

"I don't understand why you didn't get my text. I sent it an hour ago."

"Here it is! Your texts are epic. You need to make them shorter. I can't even."

"Rick said he needs a copy of the Residential Purchase Agreement."

"The RPA? Well, he can just wait for it."

"Do you want me to send it to him?"

"No. He needs to stop. There. Done."

"You sent it that fast?"

"Yes. Next?"

"Make sure Rick has a copy of the Seller in Possession Addendum."

"The SIP? Omg! He has all of this! What a moron."

"Okay, are you two going to be able to work together? Is this still about the dermatologist?"

"Yes! Rick went in for a vampire facial and he ended up dating the vampire!"

"Logan, please. If you can. Just see that Rick has all of the documents he needs."

"I will. I'm just tired of him making drama. He's been in real estate for two minutes, he doesn't know what he's doing and it's annoying!"

"Didn't Rick used to work for Coldwell Banker?"

"VC!! He used to work for Versace in Livermore! At the outlets!"

"How did Rick meet Bridgette?"

"Bridgette's Bootie is in the Versace window. They're co-branding."

"Okay. I need to sell Helen's house. Rick better not mess up this deal."

"Dead now. I cannot keep hearing his name. Can we call him something else?"

"What do you want me to call him?!"

"I don't care. Anything. Please."

"How about Donatella?"

"Perf. I'll call Donatella later. Can you text me Helen's e-mail? I need to DocuSign her the rest of the disclosures."

"You can't DocuSign Helen. She doesn't have a computer."

"Wait, what? Are you kidding me?!"

"Logan, she's never turned on her dishwasher."

"I have to drive to Helen's house every time we need her to sign a paper?"

"Either that or she has to come to the office."

"Do you know how long it took Helen get here from Napa last week? Three hours. She took the Segway!"

"I don't think Helen even has a car. You have to go this afternoon. How long will it take you?"

"I'll go. It will take me 28 minutes. Maybe I'll stop at Don Giovanni and grab a beet salad," Logan said, joking, not joking.

Bistro Don Giovanni. Best place to chill. Order the Trifle with a sharing spoon.

"That's fine," I said, "Stop at Lawler's and get Helen some malfatti. They're her favorite. I'll call her and tell her not to order any dinner."

Logan's stomach growled louder than Zeus. He talked over it and said, "Can you tell her to put Zeus in his crate? That dog is ridic. It looks like a giant hamster."

"What's ridic is this transaction. We need to keep this deal together for Helen. Before you leave the property, be sure to check the pizza oven."

"What's wrong with the pizza oven?"

"Helen got a restraining order."

"A restraining order on the pizza oven?! Deets, please."

"Yes! The lawyers are trying to get a boundary line agreement. Just make sure the pizza oven is still there."

"I can't believe Helen's having to deal with all of this. Helen loves that pizza oven."

"I know. Her husband built it. He used to fire it up and throw pizza parties with ultra-premium wines. Helen hasn't had a piece of pizza since 1979."

"Does the buyer know about the restraining order?"

"He knows. He's waiting to sign the disclosure. Remember, don't go too early. Helen doesn't get up until eleven."

That afternoon, Logan took his usual shortcut to Helen's house.

On his way from Sonoma to Napa, driving past Buena Vista Winery and alongside the symmetrical rows of bud breaking grapevines, Logan encountered a pastoral problem. There was a cow in the middle of the road. Logan called in a panic as he facepalmed and said, "OMG. You are not going to believe this. It said I was supposed to be there in 28 minutes, but there's a cow in the middle of the road! And it won't move!"

"Where are you?"

"I'm on my way to Helen's. Waze said this was the fastest route, but nobody put there was a cow!"

"Is it a cow or a bull?"

"How am I supposed to know?"

"Well, does it look like *Ferdinand*?"

"It looks just like him!"

"Then it's a bull."

"I've been sitting here for fourteen minutes!" Logan said, as he beeped his horn.

"You do realize, that your shortcut is taking you longer than if you had just gone the regular way."

"Obvi! WTF! Swerve, you bull bitz! Sorry, not sorry."

"That reminds me. Be sure to call Brigitte and see if she's attending the inspections."

"Bridgette's in Hawaii."

"I thought she confirmed. What do you mean she's in Hawaii?"

Logan laughed and said, "She went to Turtle Bay. I saw her at Blue Bottle this morning on her way to the airport."

"Bridgette went to Hawaii in the middle of our deal? What about the inspections?"

"What about them?" Logan asked.

"They're scheduled for tomorrow," I said.

"Well, we'll just have to cancel them. The buyer doesn't want inspections now. He's going for tapas at Cuca."

"He's doing what?"

Logan laughed and explained, "Going for tapas at Cuca. It's his favorite restaurant in Bali. He's taking his private jet. He's craving tapas."

"How come I haven't heard any of this? If the buyer's going Cuca, I need to know!"

Growing equally frustrated by the complete closedmindedness of a stubborn scrotumed bull who had the immediacy of slow WiFi, Logan opened his open-mindedness a little too wide.

"I'm getting out of the car," Logan said.

"Don't get out of that car, Logan."

Logan got out of his car and quickly jumped back in. "That bull is big," he said.

"Wait a minute. How do you know the buyer doesn't want inspections?"

"Donatella messaged me before I took this ROAD."

"What about Helen?" I asked.

"What about her? She'll just have to move. She'll be fine. We'll get her a gift certificate from Kokkari."

"Logan. What is she going to do, Segway to The City?! She's ninety years old. She can't move out of her house that fast."

"The struggle is real."

A boisterous bachelorette party in a Beau Sprinter limo,

that was in a line of cars stopped behind Logan, began singing "Sweet Caroline". The bride leaned her arm out the window to take a video that would go viral.

With that, my transaction coordinating millennial could not tolerate it one more second. He got out of his car a second time, determined to deal with the bull. On that country road, teaming with shortcutting, speeding millennials and Gen Zers, unknowingly and unwillingly if he had known it, Logan felt a real struggle of his own. He was, an idiom.

Logan was, on the horns of a dilemma.

Logan grabbed that bull by the horns and wrestled him to the ground.

Once on the ground, after a series of moves and countermoves and a few chops from *The Karate Kid* that he had seen for the first time at his parent's house the night before, Logan tamed his bull.

Leading with love and believing karma is a boomerang, Logan put the top down on his convertible Prius and gave the bull a ride. A ride like they were on the *Concours d' Elegance.* In a Prius. With a bull.

A Karma Revero came from behind him and flew right by him, driven by a bratty Gen Zer, in a rush to BottleRock.

# BABY BOOMER; PATSY & BOOMER

Patsy was a divorced baby boomer. When her millennial son, Taylor, moved out of her guest cottage, Patsy became an empty nester baby boomer. When he left his cat and she renamed the cat Boomer, Patsy became a baby boomer with a Boomer.

And just like that, she changed her story.

She was Patsy, but no patsy.

One day, bored with staying home and building her mystique, Patsy decided to venture out. She remembered a special invitation she had received earlier that week to an everything pet, pop-up shop.

Patsy grabbed her leopard coat and her designer sunglasses, jumped in her practical sedan, and left her real house for her wheelhouse; afternoon shopping.

She slid down in her car seat as she drove past Mary at Fideaux, Patsy's usual favorite pet boutique in downtown St. Helena.

She was tempted by the sweet smell of Oak wood and slow-cooked barbecue ribs as she passed Rutherford Grill.

She remembered the fun music of KC and The Sunshine Band at the Margrit Mondavi Summer Concert Series in Oakville.

Patsy continued driving south and arrived mid-valley at Petconi's, a fake luxury pet shop that had popped up in downtown Yountville. The pop-up had created a lot of hullabaloo. It disrupted business and traffic and left locals talking about more than just the town's yummy lemon tarts.

The parking was terrible. Patsy almost went home. Right then, she saw a spot in front of the entrance. That was a miracle, she thought to herself. The only thing was, Patsy didn't believe in miracles.

Patsy grabbed her bubble tea and almost choked on some Yountville tea, when she saw her ex-husband and his new modern millennial wife heading into the shop with their champion standard poodle. Patsy felt like throwing one of her bubbles, but maintained composure thanks to a generous amount of alimony and her hormone patch.

As Patsy entered the shop, looking for some ex-sighting healing, she was drawn to a grouping of geodes arranged on a table near a Drop-Off Aquarium. The brightest light shined from a random bowl of illuminating crystals.

Patsy picked up a crystal and asked Marcus, the holiday help millennial, what was so special about the crystals. Marcus said he didn't know. He was just there from Spain, visiting his grandmother as he did every year, and had seized the employment opportunity when it popped up.

Impressed by his motivation and still holding the crystal, Patsy wished Marcus would engage in his holiday job and be the best he could be for the time he was there.

Suddenly, a ray of blue light beamed out of the crystal in Patsy's hand and Tracked. Down. Marcus.

Marcus tossed his head back confidently and began working that pop-up store. He offered customer education. Swiped revenue generation. He even gave a demonstration. Marcus grabbed that rubber dog toy and he tossed that flying saucer!

The pet haute couture influencers invited that day stood clapping. They could not get enough of Marcus.

Patsy stood staring. She could not believe her eyes.

"That's a pretty funky crystal," Patsy said to herself, unable to deny its magic powers. She wondered what her baby boomer friends might do if they had a magic crystal.

A magic crystal that would allow them to change one thing in their life and in so doing, change their story.

As fabulous and flawless as he was, Marcus could still not identify that random bowl of crystals. Willing to negotiate, Marcus told Patsy he would happily wrap up the crystals and include them as a gift with purchase. A purchase that disguised them, so as not to alert management.

Marcus put his hands on his hips and gave a tilt of his head. A tilt towards a litter box with non-tracking crystals.

Patsy was no match for the new Marcus. Her practical side thought of Boomer and her adventurous side thought of those crystals. "Wrap up the magic crystals!" she exclaimed.

Patsy happily paid Marcus the $300. for a litter box she

knew was selling in a membership only warehouse for $99.95. The magic crystals he placed in her bag were priceless.

She thanked Marcus and told him she knew he would do well. Marcus would take his newfound celebrity back to Zara in Barcelona where he would become a fashion icon in their AR Windows.

Patsy left the store with her purchase and walked to her car. At the very moment she was about to engage in some post purchase behavior due to disbelief in magic and miracles, her son called. His ringtone was "That'll Be the Day" by Buddy Holly.

Patsy put the phone between her ear and the box and answered it, "Hello, darling. How are you?"

"Fine. You just called me three times," Taylor said.

"I did? Oh, I'm sorry. I must be pocket dialing again."

"Everything ok?"

"Yes. Just a bit flustered."

"Mom, am I on speaker phone? I hear a dog."

"You probably are. There's a lot going on here."

"Like what?" Taylor asked.

"I'll tell you when I see you. I just saw your father."

"Was he with the millennial?"

"The millennial and the poodle," Patsy said.

"Oh, the Millennidoodle," Taylor said.

"Yes," Patsy laughed.

"I have to go, mom. My flight's boarding. I'll FaceTime you from Mae Chan."

"Ok, darling. That means I probably won't talk to you until you get back, but okay. Be careful."

Taylor was a worldly and elegant millennial. He was leaving to teach ballet at a learning community in the north of Thailand. Taylor was going with his best friend, Hoang, a level-headed millennial hip-hop instructor from Vacaville. They were millennials going places and quickly, with global entry status.

"I'll post some photos on Facebook for you! Love you," he said.

"I love you, too. Thank you for calling your mother," Patsy said. Taylor missed it. He had already ended the call.

There is something about when a mother receives a phone call from her son, that not only gives her the strength to carry on, but the strength to load a heavy litter box into her car.

On her drive home to Calistoga, Patsy opened her sunroof and let in the Vitamin D. She drove by the home of her friend, Lori, whom she had known since high school. Lori waved from her driveway. Patsy threw a magic crystal out the sunroof. It tracked down that baby boomer's waving hand and lit it up. Patsy would call her later to explain.

She decided to stop at some of her usual haunts where generations were working successfully together.

Her first stop was the Napa Olive Oil Manufacturing Co. in St. Helena. It always cheered her up to see the millennial Stefano and the Contessa Ghibli. The Contessa was Stefano's 2019 Maserati Ghibli.

His family business was tri-generational and responsible for the mecca of authentic olive oils, fennel sausages, and artisan cheeses that transported you with their delicious aromas once inside that charming white barn. The walls were decorated with decades of collected business cards and original railroad tracks were set into the concrete floor.

There were picnic tables under the mature Oak trees, and they used to have a small aviary filled with doves. Patsy kind of missed those feathered friends. She would have to take a drive out to the Tides in Bodega Bay to reminisce with "The Birds".

Patsy browsed about the barn and had Stefano cut her a large piece of Teleme cheese with his wire cutter. She stocked up on long breadsticks for a dramatic look on her teak tables.

Patsy was hosting a millennial brunch the following morning with Millionaire's Bacon and Minimum Wage Eggs.

She hugged Stefano and tried to say goodbye to a fourth-generation toddler, but he was hiding behind Stefano's leg.

Embracing her inner millennial and knowing the change she was about to make in this world, Patsy waved to the Contessa as she drove off to finish her final errands.

She stopped at a local consignment shop and bought herself a consigned bucket hat. The hat was less about logos and more about the construction. It was the perfect millennial touch.

Her last stop was her baby boomer friend Alan's frame shop where, "inside a little stone building magic happens", and where Alan and his son, Chris, were busy constructing elegant frames for local wineries. She gave Alan a magic crystal because you can never have too much magic.

Patsy purchased a couple of frames to display her artist friend's "Forage from Fire" series at her brunch the following morning, and headed home.

That night, Patsy loaded Boomer into the car and headed out with her magic crystals. She drove through town putting the crystals in places her baby boomer friends were sure to find them.

When she was done and feeling the urge to drive more,

Patsy thought to herself, what about all my friends in San Francisco?

Patsy decided to keep on motoring! She drove through a brilliant baby boomer's tunnel, the Robin Williams Tunnel.

As she came out the other side, Patsy approached the Golden Gate Bridge to her San Francisco, her sun roof open to all the stars and moon above and singing karaoke to her namesake Patsy Cline.

The moon over *Baghdad-by-the-Bay* was stunning.

It was still a city to love.

Patsy had built up so much mystique, she was mystical.

She secured the bucket hat tightly on her head and the crystals securely in the passenger seat next to her. She looked in her rearview mirror at Boomer, then forward towards The City and she smiled. This baby boomer not only had a Boomer, she had a city full of friends, a son who remembered to call his mother, and she had just broadened the definition of repurposing.

▼

# YOU MUST WATCH
# *THE GREEN MILE*
# TO
# FULLY UNDERSTAND
# THIS SECTION

*The Green Mile* is not a Netflix and Chill situation. It is a movie that deserves your undivided attention, no matter how seductive the distraction. It is ripe with message.

If I had a millennial, I would tell them this: Life has flies. It just does. Because life has, what flies like. If you step in some, hose off your boots and keep walking.

The town of Sonoma is the most beautiful small town in the state of California, IMO. During summer, however, when the farmers and ranchers fertilize their fields with manure, the malodor controls the bull. And all the rest of us.

It never fails that I will get out of my car and the first thing I subconsciously do, is check the bottoms of my boots.

One time my neighbor, Myron, saw me. He stuck his head out of his Ford F-150 and hollered, "They're fertilizing!"

Don't blame yourself for a situation that's not yours.

Have great fun! Find joy! Take adventures!

You can find joy in the simplest of pleasures, the smallest of creatures, and in the face of the most overwhelming of circumstances.

I am not saying some Magic Man is going to appear out of nowhere and cure your bladder infection, although I do know a good urologist in Century City.

Happiness is something you sometimes have to work at. You have to create it. Make your happiness happen. I would want my millennial, being born into the most creative generation of all time, to understand this.

It can be as simple as a vanilla ice cream at Mitchell's.

Happiness, once you find it, must be protected. Don't let anyone step on your mouse.

Remember, you are sui generis.

I have a Silent Generation friend named Betty. I love Betty. I do. But whenever Betty calls me, she blows flies. Tells me all of her problems. And all of her friends' problems. And all of their kids' problems. She blows, and she blows, and she blows.

And when she's done, Betty tells me there's another call coming in and she has to go. She has to go and blow more flies.

And there I'm left, coughing, choking on Betty's flies.

Logan hates Betty. He asked me why I even take her calls. I said, "How can you love Inclusivity and hate Betty?" He clarified that he doesn't hate Betty, he just doesn't think it's necessary.

Maybe Logan is right. Maybe even Inclusivity would block Betty. Betty just has too many flies. No one wants to inhale them. Lately, she's had some really big ones.

Then I remembered, I love Betty. I don't talk to Betty because I feel sorry for her or because I want her Saint Christopher medal. I talk to Betty because she's a good person. She makes me laugh.

While standing in line at a physical bank branch across the street from Hank's Creekside, I stumbled upon self-awareness. I decided that I needed to set some boundaries with Betty. I needed to give myself a fly-like reminder, so that the next time she calls, I won't answer unless I'm really up for it.

I went on the internet and took a screenshot of the ultimate fly. Jeff Goldblum. I made it Betty's contact photo.

Images are destinations. Imaging is your GPS. If you can visualize where you want your life to be, what that looks like, then all you have to figure out is how to get there.

# THE SILENT GENERATION; RUTH & ROBERT

Robert was standing outside the bathroom door. Ruth was inside the bathroom with the door locked. They were in the conflict resolution portion of their morning.

The theme song to Family Feud played faintly from a television in the other room. They missed Richard Dawson, but they still loved the game show.

"Ruth, I need to get in there."

"I'm not opening the door, Robert."

"I have to go to the bathroom, Ruth."

"This isn't our bathroom anymore, Robert. It's my safe space."

"Well, then I have to go to the safe space. Open the door. What are you doing in there anyway?"

"I'm cleaning the filter."

"Forget about that stupid filter."

"I'm afraid of what I'm going to say, Robert."

"I'm afraid of what I'm going to do, Ruth, if you don't open that door."

The door opened slowly. Robert stood still and did not move. Ruth poked her head out of the bathroom, "C'mon! What's the matter, Robert?"

"I lost the urge," Robert said.

"Maybe the urge will come back. Come in and close the door," Ruth said, as she pulled Robert inside the bathroom and closed the door. Ruth stood in front of the sink and looked in the mirror. Her hair was getting long. It was time to see Anna at Sproos. Life appeared to be changing her looks by the moment. "I think I'm shrinking, Robert. Either that, or the sink is getting higher."

"Maybe I should shave before the sink gets too high," Robert said.

"Shave for what?"

"Today is the day."

"Oh, no. No, no." Ruth said.

"Yes, Ruth, I'm going to do it today. And you're coming with me."

"I'm not doing it, Robert. No!"

Robert grabbed onto Ruth's elbows. Mostly for support, but also for emphasis.

"Ruth, how long are we going to stay in here?"

"Forever. I don't like it out there."

Suddenly, a chilling ALERT sounded loudly on their

television and interrupted programming. They opened the door cautiously to listen:

**This is an alert of the Millennial Broadcast System. This is a first official statement and final warning to All Silent Generation persons. You are hereby prohibited from appearing in public without being fitted with your new Gen Y issue PCF (Politically Correct Filter): Millennial Speak Conversion Technology. Any Silent person seen without this filter properly attached and in working order will be detained, regardless of whether or not you can figure out how to turn it on. This message has been provided by the service branch of the World, the Untrained Millennial Army. The UMA now returns you to your regularly scheduled programming. Thank you and have a nice day!**

The Family Feud theme song resumed. Ruth slammed the bathroom door and locked it. She threw her back up against the door, arms and legs extended.

"It's official, Robert! Did you hear that? It's official!"

"I'm going out there," Robert said, trying to push past Ruth and open the door.

"No, Robert! Don't leave me alone in the safe space!"

"Look at us, Ruth. This used to be our bathroom. Last night you slept in here!"

"Please don't go, Robert."

"I feel uncomfortable," Robert said, holding his stomach.

"It's their fig juice, Robert. I thought the state was trying to reduce emissions. There's something figgy going on! I'm not drinking the fig juice!"

93

"I'm not staying in here, Ruth. That's what I'm not doing. I'm going to go out into my cluttered garage, get into my car that's too big for me, pull my pants up to my nose and I'm driving to the Plaza! I'm going to stand right there at the intersection, face all the cars that go by and I'm going to say what I need to say! And I'm leaving my filter at home!"

"Not tonight, Robert. It's Tuesday Night Farmers Market. There are too many people. You'll never find a place to park."

"I don't umderstand it, Ruth. Live music and crafts just to buy a tomato. Everything has to be a social event! What would their filter say about that?!"

"Don't say that, Robert. Technology is advancing every day with the help of the UMA."

"What is wrong with you, Ruth?"

"I don't know, Robert. I don't even know the difference between prompt care and urgent care anymore. If there was something wrong with me, I couldn't even get the help I needed!"

"I'm sorry, Ruth. I'm just having a bad day. Maybe I'll go mow the lawn. It might help me relax. I should have been a gardener."

"They're not called gardeners anymore, Robert. They're Lawn Estheticians. They offer grass removal services. They don't wax, they mow. They either mow it all or they leave a grass strip right down the middle of your driveway!"

"What are you talking about, Ruth?"

"I'm talking about the millennials, Robert. The millennials are changing the world!!!"

"Ruth, how long did you have that filter on? You're starting to sound like them."

"I didn't have my filter on. It's right here!"

Ruth grabbed a large black mask with a sealed cover over the nose and mouth. She looked at it and said, "I can't even get it to work right. Every time I put this damn PCF on and say, 'I hate my iPhone' it converts to playing 'Despacito'. Is it supposed to do that, Robert? Is it supposed to play music?"

"I don't know, Ruth. I don't know!"

Ruth began humming "Despacito".

"Ruth, please stop. I can't breathe."

"Should I call Jeffrey?"

"Don't call Jeffrey," Robert said, "I called him last night and our grandson answered his phone. I asked Kyle how he was enjoying his new car and he told me at least he knew how to enjoy his life! Can you believe he said that, Ruth? He didn't learn that from his father. And he didn't learn that from us. Where did he learn that, Ruth?"

"He didn't mean it, Robert."

"He's the one who needs a filter! Can you imagine if we put a filter on Kyle? One of our brand filters, Ruth. A Silent Filter!"

"Lower your voice, Robert. They'll hear you."

Robert lowered his voice and said, "Can you imagine a Silent Filter on Kyle? When he tells me 'At least I know how to enjoy my life,' it will convert to 'Let me take you for a ride in my new car, Papa. You paid for it!!'"

Ruth put her hand over her mouth and giggled her Ruth giggle.

"And our filter will be the best filter, Ruth. It will be better than the PCF. Our filter will not only change the world, it will be able to change Kyle's voice! It will make him sound like, Lawrence Welk!"

"A one and a two," Ruth reminisced.

"Lawrence Welk, Ruth! Lawrence Welk!"

"Ssshh! We need to be careful, Robert. You can't say that name. It's on the Forbidden List."

Robert hollered, "Lawrence Welk and his Champagne Music!"

"Robert, be quiet!"

"I'm in my own bathroom, Ruth. I'll say what I want to say. Just like the old days. Remember those days, Ruth? When I could keep the urge until I got into the bathroom? Before we had to wear that damn PCF!"

"Those were my favorite days too, Robert, but it's not like that anymore. It's dangerous now," Ruth said, as she finished dusting her filter.

"I'm ninety years old. What can they do to me?!" Robert asked.

"They'll take you away, that's what they'll do. They picked up Betty last night. She was having dinner with Daniel at In-N-Out Burger. No-one has heard from her since. Jeannie said, all that was left was the pickle from her combo burger."

"They picked up Betty?"

"Yes! They picked up Betty! She was apprehended for being too negative. You can't do that nowadays. It's a misdemeanor!"

Robert looked at Ruth and watched her as she put on her PCF. Although he could not hear what she was saying, he had a feeling she was saying all the wrong things on purpose, just so her failed filter would play the catchy Latin pop song.

Ruth moved from side to side in front of the mirror. She even did a little twist and spun herself around. Right into Robert.

Robert shook his head and silently left the bathroom.

Ruth tore off the filter and threw it on the floor. "Wait for me, Robert! I'm coming with you!" Ruth hollered, running after him as quickly as she could.

Robert shook his hand and Ruth grabbed it. They locked fingers and headed for the garage.

This Silent couple did not know what their potential last words might be or how they would be received. All they knew, was that they had each other for now and they couldn't stay locked in their safe space forever.

Robert did a little two-step as he turned off the lights and closed the door behind them. He still knew how to dance.

# I DIDN'T RSVP THE HOLIDAY PARTY

$A$ Christmas caroling millennial named Kimi and a caroling baby boomer named Kim, both in traditional yuletide costumes complete with cozy capelets and plaid bonnets stood by the circular driveway of the Mission Inn & Spa, the venue for my office holiday party.

As they waited for the rest of their caroling group to arrive, the caroling millennial sang an ascending scale to warm up her voice and tune her ears. It went like this:

Me-Me-Me-Me (descend) Me-Me-Me. I-I-I-I (descend) I-I-I.

I valeted my Mini Goodwood and headed into the event.

The Spanish mission style inn did not disappoint. It shined brightly this year with mini white lights and its sparkling tiered pool fountain. The Inn had a Michelin rated restaurant and was one of the few luxury resort spas in the country sourcing its own thermal mineral water.

I followed the lighted pathway into the lobby decked with hope filled trees.

I had not RSVP'd the holiday party due to general discontent, low energy levels, and the fact that my mother was having a knee manipulation that morning.

Lance and Chelle had invited me to the annual Sonoma County Christmas Bird Count at dawn. I responded right away that I could not attend. Mom's new knee was being a real Ruddy Duck!

No one expected that when Dr. Diana told my mother to go home and ice her knee, her freezer would have unexpectedly stopped freezing.

Aah, the holidays!

Brian walked up behind me as I sat by the fireplace. He tapped me on the shoulder to get my attention and wish me happy holidays. He was dressed as a wise man and had stopped to make an appearance on his way to a living nativity scene in Santa Rosa. He had plans to take the Smart Train to Hamilton afterwards and visit family.

I had been talking to a man named Nars, sitting across from me. He had brownish-red hair and wore a Tom Ford floral jacquard dinner jacket and dress pants, because he wanted to. His fragrance was unique; discreet and restrained. His legs were crossed, one slightly swinging. His eyebrows were on fleek. He stirred his spiked eggnog with a nutmeg dipped swizzle stick and talked Tesla.

Nars came across as pompous, but was sporting an egg snog, so it was difficult to take him too seriously. Somehow, he swizzled his monologue into a conversation about DNA.

"'I'm studying the origins and migrations of my haplogroup. Have you done your DNA?" Nars asked.

"'I have. I did it three times."

"'You did your DNA three times?"

"Yes."

"Why is that?"

"Well the first time, as I was preparing my saliva sample, my buffer fluid broke."

"You spilled the buffer fluid?"

"Yes. They told me the occurrence is uncommon, but it does happen occasionally. They were very nice. They sent me a new kit."

"A second kit."

"Yes. A second kit."

"What happened to that one?"

"We're not sure. They said when the laboratory attempted analysis, the concentration of DNA was insufficient to produce genotyping results."

"That's extra."

"I know. Extra Carmel Coffee Frappuccino. I don't think I waited the full thirty minutes before I gave my sample. The third time produced a result."

Nars sat upright as our #1 top-producing real estate agent entered the room. It was hard to miss her. She was distinguished-looking. Her face was like luminous silk due to good genes and Giorgio Armani's award-winning foundation. She always wore her trademark bright orange trench-coat and had a high-powered sphere of influence that included the Prime Minister of her native France. She was sharp, yet mild. She carried crackers in her purse.

Her name was Mimolette. We all knew her as Lille.

I was happy to see Lille looking so well.

She exhibited solid self-esteem and truly genuine feelings

as she hugged her fellow agents. I had heard she'd had a nervous breakdown, but it appeared only her superficial nerves had broken down.

"I have an egg snog," Nars said, as he wiped his moustache mouth.

My mobile phone vibrated. "Excuse me," I said, answering my phone, "Hello? No more ice?! Okay, I'm not staying long. I'll bring you some. Love you, too. Bye."

I ended the call and looked at Nars. "It was nice meeting you, Nars. My mother needs some ice. It's a long story."

"Aah, the maternal haplogroup. Is she okay?"

"Yes. Thank you. Happy holidays," I said, as I stood up to leave.

It became clear that the VS cognac in Nars' eggnog, not only stood for Very Special, but also Very Strong. He continued the conversation saying, "My maternal haplogroup was likely to have lived in Iran. Or was it, Scandinavia? Where was your maternal haplogroup from?"

"My maternal haplogroup traced back to a little Italian woman carrying a cooler in Clearlake. She used to walk every day of summer, down an unpaved path from our cabin and across a highway to the subdivision's pool. Sometimes she had my paternal haplogroup with her."

As I walked away, I passed Maggie and Benita wearing matching Christmas bulb necklaces they bought on Amazon prime. The Woodward Sisters were all smiles. Morgan held onto a set of Himalayan salt shot glasses, her white elephant gift.

I noticed Jared looking swag in his Saint Laurent studded bomber jacket. Jared was a newer agent who had just closed his first deal for $7 million off a floor call and was feeling bougie. He was with his famous client, hip hop legend Uncle Pinot.

"Happy holidays, Val!" Jared said as he reached out and gave me a big hug.

"Congratulations! Welcome to the jungle!" I said.

I took a mini hamburger off a passing tray and decided to head to the hosted bar for a glass of water. A mini hamburger and water. I figured that's probably all you're really entitled to when you don't RSVP.

My broker stood at the bar drinking a soda. He had a long drive home down the San Francisco Peninsula.

I ordered my drink and we clinked glasses.

My broker asked me who I was talking to by the fireplace. I looked back at Nars and saw him talking to Jared. Then I looked at my broker. Come to think of it, I didn't really know who Nars was. He could have been anyone. He could have been a corporate spy for Poppy Flower.

Poppy Flower was a multi-billion-dollar private real estate brokerage that had popped up within the last decade. They were powerful, encrypted, and sahweet. They acquired other brokerages and offered hiring bonuses in cryptocurrency and Belgian chocolate gold coins.

They were futuristic, innovative and transparent. They wore PVC transparent raincoats as part of their clear fashion uniform.

They threw elaborate parties with fancy ice sculptures and a lot of shrimp.

If you hadn't been approached by Poppy Flower, you weren't on your game.

Poppy Flower was also having their holiday party that night. It was at AT&T Park, soon to be renamed Oracle Park, home of the San Francisco Giants. Rumor had it they were putting new hires on the Trinitron.

I looked around the room to see if anyone was missing; if anyone had left the company. I found myself stopping on the familiar faces of friends.

There were some pretty awesome people in that room.

I looked at Tonia and Thierry. How gorgeous were they? They let me Hang out at their home, on their sofa with my beautiful 107-pound Black Russian Terrier, Lara, for five nights during the wildfire evacuations. Tonia even cooked dinner for me. I would have to give her a hug.

You find out who your friends are, when life hands you a FEMA scale emergency.

"These pumps are killing me!" Lille said, as she walked up and grabbed my arm, "I went to Winter Walk in Union Square today and the millennials were twirling me in the green space."

"You twirled in those pumps on AstroTurf?"

"It's green space now."

"You would know, Lille. You live in green space."

"Not this year. I didn't hit my goal," Lille said.

Humility, I thought to myself. Maybe Lille had changed.

Lille kicked off her pump and began massaging her foot as she disclosed, "17,000 square feet of green space. We twirled for 11,000 square feet of it! Then they twirled me into an open-air beer garden. I had a Campfire Stout and a Luponic Distortion!"

I looked down at Lille's pump on the floor. It was a leopard print calf hair pump with a red sole that was a symbol of wealth and closed deals.

Lille and her former business partner, Kristin, always wore red soled pumps.

I noticed Ed was missing at the party. He was our computer ninja millennial agent, so tech-savvy, Tim Cook once called him with a question. Ed kept us all together. I asked Lille, "Where's Ed?"

"Ed went to Poppy Flower."

"Ed went to Poppy Flower?!"

"Yes. He just left. He went to pick up Kristin from the Poppy Flower party. She said the culture wasn't for her. She told Ed to meet her across the street in the parking lot of Momo's."

Kristin's sphere of affluence included a lot of Silent Generation clients who owned property in Pacific Heights and Cow Hollow. Apparently, many of them had complained that her new brokerage was too confusing. Poppy Flower's new building had a biometric, two-factor authentication security system with across-the-board appeal. In order to enter, not only did you have to give face recognition, but you had to give verbal praise.

"I can't believe Kristin went to Poppy Flower in the first place," I said.

"I can. They even recruited Kristin's father," Lille said.

"Otis? He's 93 years old!"

"They don't care. He still has his broker's license."

"Did they offer him a hiring bonus?"

"No, I think they're just giving him a case of applesauce."

"This is Crazytown! They left me a voicemail, but I never called them back. I'm sure Poppy Flower called you."

"Of course they called me. The Head of Poppies called me before he called Kristin," Lille said, "I sold $500 million worth of property last year. With no team! And I did my own files!"

Humility had left the building.

As Lille went to remove her other pump, she became unsteady and slipped on a commercial rubber mat behind the bar. Lille flew, right out of her shoe. She hit the wall and fell softly on the mat.

"Oh, no! Lille! Are you OK?!"

Apparently, Lille had had some Very Strong eggnog herself. Slurring her words, she asked, "Is that me on the Trinitron?"

"No, Lille, you're not on the Trinitron."

"Yes, that's me! They spelled my name wrong."

"No. Lille. You're at the holiday party."

"Call Ed to come get me! I don't want a billion dollars!"

"Yes, you do, Lille. You're coming around," I said, helping her up.

"I don't want to go to Floppy Power. I love my brand. I love my brand. I love my brand," Lille said, slightly dizzy as she stood up and opened her eyes.

"Would you like some water?" I asked.

"No. Just tell me where we are."

"We're at the Mission Inn."

"Okay. Good."

"We're doing a deal together in the Ranch, remember?"

"Right. You better close it."

"I will," I said.

Just then, the president of the company, followed by a photographer, passed by the bar. Never did a person recover so quickly.

"Merci beaucoup. Merry Christmas!" Lille exclaimed, as

she double kissed me and went off in hot pursuit, symbols of wealth in hand.

"Merry Christmas," I said.

My mobile phone vibrated, but l didn't answer. It was my friend Kate. She had missed the party. She was at Shen Yun.

As I walked out of my holiday office party and down a long hallway, I remembered when my friend and I took my mother to see Shen Yun for her birthday. It was playing at "San Francisco's Architectural Crown", the War Memorial Opera House.

I remembered the millennial who sat next to me with the screw cap wine, having trouble with her screw cap, during a quiet part of the performance.

I remembered the beautiful music made by the Erhu, an instrument with only two strings.

"What type of car do you have?" the millennial valet asked, as I stood daydreaming by the valet stand outside the Mission Inn. I looked, but couldn't find my ticket. As I retraced my steps back into the lobby, I saw a Gen X event planner named Debbie, near one of the event rooms.

Debbie was carrying what appeared to be part of a reindeer ice sculpture. Fiona and Quentin strolled out of the event room after her.

"Thanks again, Debbie," they said, "You did an amazing job. Everything was perfect."

"Thank you," Debbie said, "Happy Anniversary!"

I noticed my valet ticket on the floor by the event room. I walked over and picked it up.

"You're lucky you found that," Debbie said.

"I know. What's that you're carrying?" I asked.

"Well, it was a reindeer. Now it's just a hoof."

"Where are you taking it?"

"I was going to leave it outside by a tree," Debbie said, making a small, but nonetheless effort to care for the earth.

"Would it be possible for me to buy it from you?" I asked, "I know it's a strange request, but my mom is supposed to be icing her knee and her freezer's broken."

"Well, that's irony for you. Sure! Let me put it in a bag," Debbie said, as she grabbed a small plastic bag off her cart and struggled to make the hoof fit. I noticed her alternating Rosie red and green painted fingernails.

"I like your nails," I said.

"Oh, thank you. It was supposed to be a relaxing manicure this afternoon, but it didn't turn out that way."

"What happened?"

"The lady sitting in the pedicure chair next to me was eating six crab cake bites and a pig in a blanket. You know, the little mini crescent dog."

"At the nail salon?"

"Yes! Can you believe it?"

"What is wrong with people?"

"She's so skinny, too. She's just a foodie."

"You know the woman??"

"I do. I didn't want to say anything, but she was talking a lot with her hands and panko crumbs were flying everywhere. I had them in my hair! It kind of wrecked the experience."

"I don't know what to say."

"Here we go," Debbie said, as she got the hoof in the bag, "Yes, I hope I can keep a straight face when I see her at Broadway Market. She's always in there. It's her favorite market in Sonoma."

"Well, at least your nails are fun!"

"Yes, I like them, too."

"Thank you so much. Now I don't have to stop. My mom lives nearby," I said, reaching for my purse.

"No charge. Tell her to feel better!"

"I will. Thanks again."

"Let me bring it to your car for you," Debbie offered.

As we walked through the lobby and out to the valet counter, past the caroling KimKim's and all of that hope, I felt content.

There is a lot of good in the world.

There are people like Debbie, who not only give a hoof, but they offer to carry it to your car.

I realized that sometimes you don't need fancy ice sculptures. Sometimes, you just need some ice.

# FOUR TRIPS TO LOS GATOS

I was on my way to San Jose. I knew the way. We traveled on Highway 280, my mother's favorite since they built it. Approximately nine miles south of San Jose, I took the Highway 17 exit and veered west to the foothills of the Santa Cruz Mountains. To the unincorporated town of Los Gatos.

The first time I took this trip, I was uncertain if I would ever live to tell about it.

It was a winter storm to beat all winter storms. Something had taken over that majestic mountain.

A big bad monster had ahold of that mountain. A monster without a soul. A monster that was very upset about something.

I thought how sad it was. Everyone loved that mountain. It had gorgeous vistas, clear water streams, hiking trails, and pretty Briseyda and Marisanta flowers. It stood upright and free.

A wildflower kept on blooming.

A Renner Eagle soared.

I didn't recognize the mountain that day. The mountain had shapeshifted. It was no longer in Tadasana.

The intense coastal winds blew torrential rains and hail, whipping them mercilessly around the blind curves of that treacherous road.

It was dark and heady. I could barely see where I was going.

I looked at my mother in the passenger seat. How in the world did I get her involved in all of this?

The wind howled like a rage filled coyote with a wide-open mouth, atop an all-time high mountain above the sparkling waters of the Pacific Ocean and the brilliance of the Bay Area.

The monster boomed its loud thunderous voice and the mountain disappeared. It was ghosted by the fog.

I was alone.

I had to take care of myself and my mother now.

I slowed down. Took it easy.

The road climbed to an altitude of approximately 3,000 feet with no guard rails. I remember calling Susan and asking her if she could drive down to meet us and take us up to the barn. She told me the millennial vet tech, Alex, had just driven up and made it.

I wanted to quit and go home. I remembered what my cousin's husband, Ben, told me a long time ago. I wasn't a quitter.

There was no looking back. It was time to make my own life complete. Time to do some beautiful stuff. Enough being sidetracked.

There would be three more trips after that one. Each time, the weather getting a little better. No wind, no rain.

I could see blue sky behind the breaking clouds. A ray of sunshine streamed through the windshield and warmed my hand on the steering wheel. It made my hand hot and got my attention.

The road wasn't as scary. I knew where the curves were; it wasn't going to throw me any.

The Fed Ex truck came down the mountain and around the corner rather quickly, as if it had made the trip a million times. This was obviously his route. He was a happy millennial Fed Ex driver who had personalized his delivery experience with the sound of urban pop music on his truck stereo.

Sir Elton John's "Your Song" took me up that mountain.

He stopped his truck when he saw me and began to formulate a plan. I knew from traffic school days that the burden was on the vehicle coming down the hill to back up.

I lifted his burden and Italian Jobbed the Mini onto a narrow shoulder. The Fed Ex team member waved and screamed, "Thank U!" next to my car as he carried on down the road.

My mother hung onto the grab handle in the ceiling with her right hand and in her left hand she clutched a box of See's candies, the Silent Generation secret. She let go of the handle and made the sign of the cross.

"Why are you making the sign of the cross?" I asked.

"I'm just so very grateful," she said.

I always tried to include my mother, even when she protested. It was part of the process. When it comes to love, if you are blessed to have good people in your life, you have to be a Navy Seal. Leave no one behind.

I remember the Running of the Millennials in San Juan

Capistrano. Everyone was rushing to their wedding receptions all at the same time and my mother and I got so caught up, we ended up at the wrong reception. As our groom jokingly put it, "I bet they had better hors d'oeuvres."

My mobile phone rang. It was Susan. I answered via Bluetooth. "Hi, Susan," I said.

"Hi! Are you close?"

"Yes. We're almost there."

"Okay. The gate is open. I'll meet you at the barn."

"See you in two minutes."

"See you there! Bye."

"Ciao."

Six elegant, thickly coated white and badgered Great Pyrenees dogs stood on the sloped terrain inside the enclosure. They barked commandingly and in unison as we arrived.

They are the kindest dogs when they're your protector. They are as stubborn as mules, because they think they ALWAYS know best, but their instincts are good.

The Great Pyrs watched over all of the animals in their kingdom. They would guard an apple if it fell off their tree. They made you feel safe.

There were no horses here. This was an alpaca ranch; not open to the public. Home to the most superior fibered, color championship and blue-ribbon winning alpacas in the state.

The alpacas stood gracefully, watching. They were fabulous. Their halters were all different colors from the House of Ileana and the tufts of hair on their heads were blown out with hair dryers, San Andreas style; horizontally displaced.

They had Ivy League temperaments with undergraduate

degrees in human thinking. They craned their long necks in curiosity.

We didn't see Susan. She must be inside the barn. We walked through an entrance in the tall, rolled barbed wire fencing that lead to the closed barn doors. I reached out and grabbed the massive antique door handle, shipped home from a trip to County Cork.

This was no ordinary barn. This was a magic barn. It was spectacular. And it was huge. The barn was approximately 25,000 square feet.

I opened the barn door, slowly.

"Don't Stop Believin'" by Journey, played softly on the sound system.

Al Paca, an alpaca barista, stood by a coffee cart. He greeted us and offered a beverage. He had a twinkle in his eye.

"Hi, Al," I said, "No, thank you. I have my green tea in the car. Is Susan around?"

"She's over by the puppies," he said as he raised his sure-footed foot made up of two toes and pointed it towards the middle of the barn.

The barn had energy efficient upgraded lighting systems, so it was easy to see the way.

A giant Swarovski jellyfish chandelier stylishly hung in the entrance for ambiance, with long tentacles sending Sparkles of light everywhere.

We walked excitedly, my mother eating her milk chocolate Bordeaux.

We passed the young millennial poet, Leo, reading his latest verse to Ms. Fulton and four little Gen Zers; Evelyn, Aria, Decky, and Vincenzo in his PJs. They sat cross legged on good quality hay strewn about the barn floor. A puppy licked their silly, giggling faces. Even Ms. Fulton's!

A vet assistant known as Patrick, soon to have his own YouTube channel, sat on a stool near a heat lamp and listened to a puppy's healthy heartbeat.

Exchange students from Hamburg, Germany took selfies.

An alpaca was in Downward-Facing Dog and stayed present. She had a sense of ease and was in perfect alignment, her energy flowing. She kept her eyes on her mat, quieted her mind and she breathed her powerful alpaca breath. Her name was Tina.

Tina was pleased because her long-distance relationship was working with Dahli Llama. He had just arrived at SFO from Holly Lane Gardens on Bainbridge Island and was eagerly on his way.

There was no ego in that barn. There were no shrinking violets.

There was mindfulness.

There was Hump-free the camel's spirit.

There was Amy from Saratoga.

I looked at the eight adorable Great Pyrenees puppies running about with all the beauty of life, investigating and chewing on everything.

I was confident I would see Big Boy, but he wasn't there.

Big Boy was the first puppy I spotted, the very first time I walked into that barn. I was drawn right to him. I remember pointing to him and asking, "Who's that?"

He was the pick of the litter and two pounds heavier than any of the other puppies at birth. At eight weeks old, he already weighed 24 pounds.

A well cared for baby boomer named Susan stood up from

her portable camping chair where she was finishing a text to her Stepmother. SHE gave us warm hugs and asked, "How are you? How's the new knee?"

"It's been a challenge," my mother said.

"Would you like to sit down?" Susan asked, "I think that's the first time I've sat down since the puppies were born."

"Thank you," my mother said, "My physical therapist told me my knee was the stubbornest knee he's ever dealt with."

"You're doing great. You'll get there," Susan said.

Susan pushed you to be your near perfect self. Set the bar high. Reach. Grow. She was used to cheering on her team.

Susan had six sons. I am certain they were the source of her great inner strength. She was indeed an awesome person. I was grateful to have met her. She will never know how much she helped me during that difficult chapter of my life.

"I brought you a bottle of wine," I said, handing her the bottle.

"Thank you. You're always bringing gifts. Oh, and look, it has such a cute ornament tied to it," Susan said.

"It's from the Kris Kringle shop in Carmel-by-the-Sea. We went there as fire refugees."

"Do you have a place there?" Susan asked.

"No. My friend Carrie owns Hofsas House. It just felt so good to breathe in the scent of those sinus-opening Eucalyptus trees! Have a pretzel at Brophy's," I said.

"Our next-door neighbors beeped at us in the crosswalk. There were so many people from our town there," my mother added.

"I have nothing for you," Susan said.

"You and this barn. I will never forget you."

"You've been here to look at the puppies so many times. I'm going to miss you. Have you decided?"

"I think it would be good for Lara to have some company. Maybe a little brother. Whatever happened to Big Boy?"

"He's here."

"He is?"

"I hid him in the water closet," Susan said, "The breeders came early this morning and they all wanted him. They offered me double the cost. I saved him for you, if you want him. The first time you came in the barn, you went right to him." Susan walked to the front of the barn and opened a door off to the side.

Every single movement in that barn froze.

My life was about to change.

The door flew open with a force so playful and powerful, the door hit the back wall. The LEDs flickered. The jellyfish popped a tentacle!

Big Boy jogged past me, then back to me, then fell over and rolled on his back, kicking his big bunny feet. He made a series of funny grunts.

"Be sure to listen, the day he speaks to you," Al Paca said.

"I will," I said.

"What are you going to name him?" Susan asked.

"I'm going to name him the letter 'C'."

"C?" she questioned.

"Yes. Have you seen the movie, *A Bronx Tale?* It's also a Broadway musical."

"It's with Robert DeNiro," Al Paca said, "He's a bus driver."

"Yes!" I said.

"I've never seen it," Susan said.

"It's an amazing movie by Chazz Palminteri. The main character is named C. Robert DeNiro plays his father," I said, glancing at Al Paca, "The father tells his son, 'The saddest thing in life is wasted talent.'"

"It sounds wonderful," Susan said, "My husband and I will watch it tonight on Netflix. It's date night. We don't have the grandkids."

"Does the puppy need any special food?" My mother asked.

"I put some food in a container. I wrote down the brand name in his folder. Al, would you grab it for them?"

Susan opened the barn doors and we stepped outside. C ran out, followed by his best friend and littermate. I felt bad that I could not take them both, but I knew C was the one.

Jen and Cory, two friends in fintech, would eventually adopt C's littermate.

C was magical. He had a twinkle in his eye. He would turn out to be my spirit guide.

Susan leaned down, picked up that big boy and carried him to our car. My mother got in the front seat, and I covered her legs with a red plaid wool blanket. We put C on her lap. He slept all the way home.

We would go a different way. The Bay Bridge to the Richmond Bridge. Catching a sunset over Treasure Island is a natural treasure.

Catching a glimpse of the Novato mayor heading south after Super Bowl LIII to deliver a gift basket to the San Mateo City Council, is Bay Area good sportsmanship.

As we left Susan, Al and the alpacas, the imposing, guarding Great Pyrs and that glorious barn on the top of that mountain, I looked at my mother and said, "I think I'm going to cry."

My mother reached in her coat pocket and as she pulled out a tissue, a small fortune fell on the floor. She leaned over as best she could and picked it up. My mother handed me the fortune and said, "Here. It's the fortune from your fortune cookie at Kirin's the other night."

My hands held on tightly to the steering wheel. "I can't read it right now. I'm turning around," I said, "Read it to me."

"Your dreams are never silly. Depend on them to guide you."

In my story, the story I changed by writing this book, I dared to dream again. I let my dreams and C guide me. Dreams that weren't silly. Dreams I depended on.

Any mountain can rise and be grand again.

You can be whatever you want to be, if you put your mind to it.

## The Beginning.

# EPILOGUE

Dear Millennials,

Thanks for reading!

I'll keep it short.

See you out there! Say "Hi", or I will.

Best,

*Valerie*

Valerie

Printed in the United States
By Bookmasters

Printed in the United States
By Bookmasters